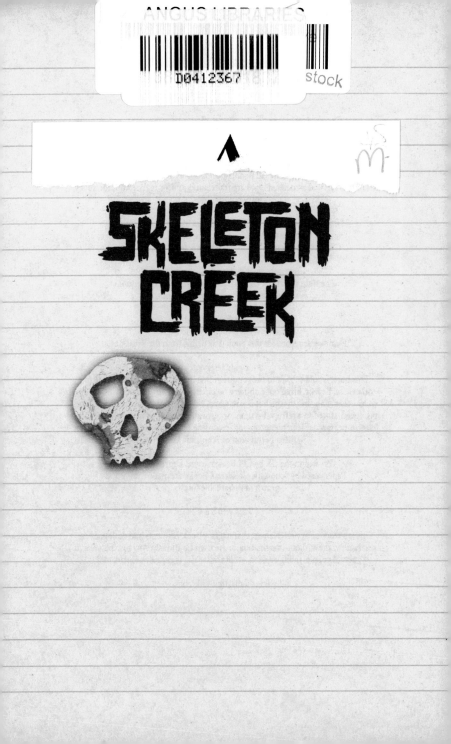

SKELETON CREEK

Scholastic Children's Books
An imprint of Scholastic Ltd
Euston House, 24 Eversholt Street
London, NW1 1DB, UK
Registered office: Westfield Road, Southam, Warwickshire, CV47 0RA
SCHOLASTIC and associated logos are trademarks and/or registered trademarks
of Scholastic Inc.

First published in the US in two volumes as *Skeleton Creek* and
Ghost in the Machine by Scholastic Inc., 2009
This edition published in the UK by Scholastic Ltd, 2010

Text copyright © Patrick Carman, 2009
The right of Patrick Carman to be identified as the author
of this work has been asserted by him.

ISBN 978 1407 11547 4

A CIP catalogue record for this book is available from the British Library.

Printed in the UK by CPI Bookmarque, Croydon, Surrey.
Papers used by Scholastic Children's Books are made from wood
grown in sustainable forests.

1 3 5 7 9 10 8 6 4 2

www.scholastic.co.uk/zone

BOOK ONE

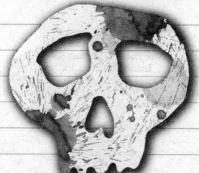

SKELETON CREEK

Patrick Carman

PC STUDIO

SCHOLASTIC

Monday, September 13, 5:30 a.m.

There was a moment not long ago when I thought: <u>This is it</u>. <u>I'm dead</u>.

I think about that night all the time and I feel the same fear I felt then. It happened two weeks ago, but fourteen days and nights of remembering have left me more afraid and uncertain than ever.

Which I guess means it isn't over yet. Something tells me it may never truly be over.

Last night was the first time I slept in my own room since everything happened. I'd got into the habit of waking in the hospital to the sound of a nurse's shuffling feet, the dry chalk-dust smell of her skin, and the soft shaking of my shoulder.

<u>The doctor will visit you in a moment</u>. <u>He'll want you awake</u>. <u>Can you sit up for me, Ryan?</u>

There was no nurse or doctor or chalky smell this morning, only the early train crawling through town to wake me at half past five. But in my waking mind, it wasn't a train I heard. It was something more menacing, trying to sneak past in the early dawn, glancing down the dead-end streets, hunting.

I was scared — and then I was relieved — because my overactive imagination had settled back into its natural resting state of fear and paranoia.

In other words, I was back home in Skeleton Creek.

Usually when the morning train wakes me up, I go straight to my desk and start writing before the rest of the town starts to stir. But this morning — after shaking the idea that something was stalking me — I had a sudden urge to leap from my bed and jump on board the train. It was a feeling I didn't expect and hadn't the slightest chance of acting on. But still, I wondered where the feeling had come from.

Now, I've rested this journal on a TV tray with its legs torn off, propped myself up in bed on a couple of pillows, and have started doing the one thing I can still do that has always made me feel better.

I have begun to write about that night and all that comes after.

Monday, September 13, 6:03 a.m.

I need to take breaks. It still hurts to write. Physically, mentally, emotionally — it seems like every part of me is broken in one way or another. But I have to start doing this again. Two weeks in the hospital without a journal left me starving for words.

I have kept a lot of journals, but this one is especially important for two reasons. Reason number one: I'm not writing this for myself. I'm putting these words down for someone else to find, which is something I never do. Reason number two: I have a strong feeling this will be the last journal I ever write.

My name, in case someone finds this and cares to know who wrote it, is Ryan. I'm almost old enough to drive. (Although this would require access to a car, which I lack.) I'm told that I'm tall for my age but need to gain weight or there's no hope of making the varsity cut next year. I have a great hope that I will remain thin.

I can imagine what this morning would have been like before the accident. I would be getting ready for the hour-long bus ride to school. I would have so much to say to Sarah. An hour next to her was always time well-spent. We had so much in common, which kept us from going completely crazy in a town populated by just under seven hundred people.

I'm really going to miss those conversations with Sarah. I wonder if I'll get lonely. The truth is, I don't even know if I'm allowed to mention her name. But I can't stop. I am a writer. This is what I do. My teachers, parents, even Sarah — they all say I write too much, that I'm obsessive about it. But then, in the same breath, they can't help but mention that I'm gifted. Like when Mrs Garvey told me I understand words and their usage in the same way a prodigy on the piano understands notes and sounds. But I have a much simpler answer, and I'm pretty sure I'm more right than my teacher is: I have written a lot, every day, every year, for many years in a row.

Practice makes perfect.

I think my favourite writers are those who admitted while they were still alive that they couldn't live without writing. John Steinbeck, Ernest Hemingway, Robert Frost — guys who put writing up there in the same category as air and water. Write or die trying. That kind of thinking agrees with me.

Because here I am. Write or die trying.

If I turn back the pages in all the journals I've written, I basically find two things: scary stories of my own creation and the recording of strange occurrences in Skeleton Creek. I can't say for certain why this is so, other than to fall back on the old adage that a writer writes what he knows, and I have known fear all my life.

I don't think I'm a coward — I wouldn't be in the position I'm in now if I was a coward — but I am the sort of person who overanalyses, worries, frets. When I hear a noise scratching under the bed — either real or imagined — I stare at the ceiling for hours and wonder what it might be that's trying to claw its way out. (I picture it with fangs, long bony fingers, and bulging red eyes.) For a person who worries like I do and has a vivid imagination to match, Skeleton Creek is the wrong sort of place to endure childhood.

I know my writing has changed in the past year. The two kinds of writing — the made-up scary stories and the documenting of events in Skeleton Creek — have slowly become one. I don't have to make up stories any longer, because I'm more certain than ever that the very town I live in is haunted.

This is the truth.
And the truth, I've learned, can kill you.

I'm tired now. So tired.
I have to put this down.
Even if I can't stop thinking about it.

Monday, September 13, 2:00 p.m.

I have to be careful to keep this hidden.

I have to make sure nobody sees me writing in it.

They're curious enough as it is.

They're watching me enough as it is.

I'm a captive, really. I'm imprisoned in my own room.

I have no idea how much they know.

I don't even know how much I know.

I have so many questions, and no way to answer them.

There is something about having been gone for two weeks in a row that helps me see Skeleton Creek with fresh eyes. I have a new idea of what someone from the outside might think if they drove into my isolated hometown where it sits alone at the bottom of the mountains.

I like to act on these thoughts and write them down as if they are occurring. It's a curious habit I can't seem to break. Maybe things are safer when I think of them as fiction.

If I imagine myself as a person arriving in Skeleton Creek for the first time it goes something like this:

7

The sun has barely risen when a car door opens and a man stands at the kerb looking out into the forest beyond the edge of town. There is a grey fog that hangs thick and sticky in the trees, unwilling to leave, hiding something diabolical in the woods. He gets back in his car and locks the doors, glancing down side streets through dusty windows. He wonders what has brought this little town to its knees. The place is not dead; it is not even dying for certain. Instead, the driver thinks to himself, this place has been forgotten. And he senses something else. There are secrets buried here that are best left alone.

It is then that the car turns sharply and leaves in the direction from which it came, the driver confident that the growing light of day will not shake the unforeseen dread he feels about the town at the bottom of the mountain.

The driver would not know exactly what it was that scared him off, but I know. Sarah knows, too. We know there's something wrong with this place, and more important, we know we're getting too close to whatever it is.

Someone's coming.

Monday, September 13, 4:30 p.m.

When did our search begin?

If I could get to my old journals, I might be able to figure out the exact date. But they're hidden, and there's no way for me to get to them in my present state. Not without help. And the only person who could help me — Sarah — isn't here any more.

I guess our searching began with a question she asked me last summer.

"Why Skeleton Creek?"

"You mean the name?"

"Yes, the name. Why call a town Skeleton Creek? Nobody wants to visit a place with a name like that. It's bad for tourism."

"Maybe the people who named it didn't want any visitors."

"Don't you think it's weird no one wants to talk about it? It's like they're hiding something."

"You're just looking for a reason to go snooping around with your camera."

"There's something to it. A name like that has to come from somewhere."

I remember thinking there was a story hidden within what she'd said, and that I wanted to be the one to write the story. I had visions of everyone in Skeleton Creek applauding my efforts to uncover the past. The fantasy of creating something important appealed to me.

We began our quest at the local library, a gloomy four-by-four-metre room at Elm and Main, open on Mondays and Wednesdays. It was also open on New Year's Day, Christmas Day, and Easter Sunday, because according to Gladys Morgan, our prehistoric and very unhappy town librarian, "Nobody comes in on those days and the library is deathly quiet, as a library should be."

Gladys Morgan is not a friendly woman. She stares at each person she encounters in precisely the same way: as if everyone in town has just kicked her cat across the room. She has skin like crumpled newspaper. Her lower lip has lost its spring and hangs heavy over her chin. There is an alarming overbite.

I remember the day we walked into the library, the little bell tinkling at our entry.

The room smelled musty, and I wasn't certain if it came from the old books or from the woman who guarded them. Sarah peppered Gladys with questions as I ran my fingers along the spines of the most boring books I'd ever seen, until at last Miss Morgan put her hand up and spoke.

"This town wasn't called Skeleton Creek until 1959."

She reached beneath her desk, which had sat decaying in the same spot for a hundred years, and pulled out a wooden milk crate. Inside were newspapers, torn and yellowed.

"You're not the first to ask about the past, so I'll advise you like I've done the rest."

She glanced past the dark curtains to the street outside and shoved the box across the desk, leaving a streak where dust had been lifted. She had a peculiar, superstitious look on her face.

"Read them if you want, but let it go after that. Beyond these you'll only stir up trouble."

Gladys took a white cloth from her pocket and removed her wire-rimmed glasses, wiping them with wrinkled hands and casting shadows across the peeling wallpaper behind her.

"I'll make a note you've checked those out. Have them back on Monday or it's a dollar a day."

The town librarian clammed up after that, as if someone had been eavesdropping and she'd said as much as she was allowed to. But Gladys Morgan had given us a beginning, a thread to grab hold of. It would lead us to trouble of a kind we hadn't anticipated.

Monday, September 13, 6:40 p.m.

I stopped there for a while because all of this has made me think of Sarah.

I wonder, if she were here, whether she'd be telling what happened the same way. Not writing it down — "Not my thing," she always said. But I wonder if she would remember things differently.

I look back, I see warning signs.

Sarah looks back, she sees invitations.

I miss her.

I blame her.

I'm scared for her.

I'm scared _of_ her. Not a lot. But some.

It was wrong of me to write "I blame her."

It's not like she tricked me into anything.

I went along willingly.

I was the one who put my life on the line. Even if I didn't realize I was doing it.

I guess what I'm saying is that none of this would have happened if Sarah hadn't been around.

Now—

I do miss her.

And I do blame her.

And I'm sure her story would be different from mine.

But where was I? Oh, yeah — we began reading through the stack of newspapers. From 1947 to 1958, there had been a paper for the 1,200 residents. The paper had an uninspiring name — *The Linkford Bi-Weekly* — but it told us what our town had once been called. Linkford. It had a nice ring to it, or so I thought at the time.

The title of the paper became more interesting in 1959 when it was renamed *The Skeleton Creek Irregular.* (This was an appropriate name, for we could only find a handful of papers dated between 1959 and 1975, when the publisher fled to Reno, Nevada, and took the printing press with him.)

Linkford sat alone on a long, empty road at the bottom of a forested mountain in the western state of Oregon. It surprised us to discover that an official from the New York Gold and Silver Company had suggested the town name be changed to Skeleton Creek. Actually, we were fairly dumbstruck that anyone from New York would take an interest in our town at all.

"Why in the world would a big city mining company want to change the name of the town?" I remember asking Sarah.

"It's that monstrous machine in the woods," she answered. "The dredge. I bet that has something to do with it. They probably owned it."

The dredge. Already, we were headed towards the dredge. I'll bet Sarah was planning things in her mind even way back then.

Not knowing the consequences.

Just thinking about the mystery.

We pieced together the small bits of information we could gather from those who would talk (hardly anyone) and the newspapers we'd been given (less than thirty in all, none complete editions). We had gone as far as creepy old Gladys Morgan said we should go, and yet we kept pulling on the thread we'd taken hold of.

Of course, I was less enthusiastic than Sarah at first, knowing that if our parents discovered what we were doing, they would demand that we stop prying into other people's business. Privacy has long been the religion of our town.

But Sarah can be persuasive, especially when she finds

something she wants to record on film. She could be consumed by filmmaking in the same way that I am with writing. Our creative obsessions seem to draw us together like magnets, and I had a hard time pulling away when she was determined to drag me along.

And so we kept digging.

Of course, I know where all of this is going.
I just have to get it down on paper.
One last time.

Monday, September 13, 8:30 p.m.

Remember.

I have to try to remember all the details. They could still be important.

It feels like midnight: it's only 8:30.

How did this happen to me?

Stop, Ryan. Go back.

Remember.

Even if you know how it's going to feel.

Even if you don't have any of the answers.

There were small announcements in four of the newspapers that alluded to something called the Crossbones. They were cryptic ads in nature, containing a series of symbols and brief text that seemed to have no meaning. One such message read as follows: <u>The floor and 7th, four past the nine on door number two.</u> Crossbones. Who in their right mind could decipher such nonsense? Certainly not us.

All of the advertisements came between the years of 1959 and 1963 and all appeared in *The Skeleton Creek Irregular.* Then, in 1964, they ceased altogether, as if they had never existed at all. But the same symbols could still be found in various places. One of the symbols — two bones tangled in barbed wire — could be seen above the door to the local bar, on a signpost at the edge of town, and again carved into a very old tree along a pathway into the woods. It made us wonder if the members of the Crossbones were still meeting. Who had been part of the society? What was its function? Were there still active members — and, if so, who were they?

Our trail dead-ended with the advertisements.

We searched relentlessly online for clues to our town's past. New York Gold and Silver was bankrupted over environmental lawsuits, and it seemed to vanish into thin air after 1985. But this didn't keep us from sneaking down the dark path into the woods to examine what was left behind.

Do I wish we'd never gone down that path?

Yes.

No.

I don't know.

It's too complicated.

Or is it? None of this would have happened if we'd stayed away from the dredge.

The dredge is a crucial part of the town's dreary

past. It sits alone and unvisited in the deepest part of the dark woods. The dredge, we discovered, was a terrible machine. Its purpose was to find gold, and its method was grotesque. Twenty-four hours a day, 365 days a year, the dredge sat in a muddy lake of its own making. It dug deep into the earth and hauled gargantuan buckets of stone and debris into itself. Nothing escaped its relentless appetite. Everything went inside the dredge. Trees and boulders and dirt clods the size of my head were sifted and shaken with a near-deafening racket, and then it was all spat out behind in piles of rubble three metres high. A tail of ruin — miles and miles in length — all so tiny bits of gold could be sifted out.

The trench that was left behind as the dredge marched forward formed the thirty-five-kilometre streambed that zigzags wildly along the edge of town and up into the low part of the mountain. The gutted earth filled with water, and the banks were strewn with whitewashed limbs that looked like broken bones.

The new waterway torn from earth and stone was called Skeleton Creek by a man in a suit from New York. Maybe it had been a joke, maybe not. Either way the name stuck. Soon after, the town took the name as well. It would seem that New York Gold and Silver held enough sway over Linkford to change the town name to whatever it wanted.

The greatest discovery — or the worst, depending on how you look at it — that Sarah and I made involved the untimely death of a workman on the dredge. There was only one mention of the incident in the newspaper, and nothing anywhere else. Old Joe Bush is what they called him, so I can only conclude that he was not a young man. Old Joe Bush had let his trouser leg get caught in the gears, and the machinery of the dredge had pulled him through, crushing his leg bone into gravel. Then the dredge spat him out into the grimy water. His leg was demolished, and under the deafening sound in the dark night, no one heard him scream.

Old Joe Bush never emerged from the black pond below.

Monday, September 13, 10:00 p.m.

OK. I think everyone is asleep now.
 It's as safe as it's going to get.

Late last night, on my arrival home from the hospital, I
was reunited with my computer. This may seem like a
strange thing to write, but the already walloping power
of a computer is magnified even more for people like me
in a small, isolated town. It is the link to something not
boring, not dull, not dreary. It has always been especially
true in my case because Sarah is constantly making videos,
posting them, and asking me to take notice.
 One simple click — that's all it can take for your life
to change.
 Sometimes for the better.
 Sometimes for the much worse.
 But we don't think about that.
 No, we just click.
 There is a certain video she made fifteen days ago,
a day before the accident. This video is like a road sign
that says YOU'VE GONE TOO FAR. TURN BACK. I am
afraid to look at it again, because I know that after I

watch it, I'm going to have even more of a bewildering sense that my life has been broken into two parts — everything that came before this video, and everything that would come after.

As much as I don't want to, I'm going to stop writing now. There is a safety in writing late into the night, but I can't put off watching it again. I have to see it once more, now that things have changed for the worse.

It might help me.

It might not.

But I have to do it.

I have to.

I'm afraid.

It's so simple. Just go to Sarah's name online. Sarahfincher.com. Enter the password houseofusher. Then click return.

One click.

Do it, Ryan.

Do it.

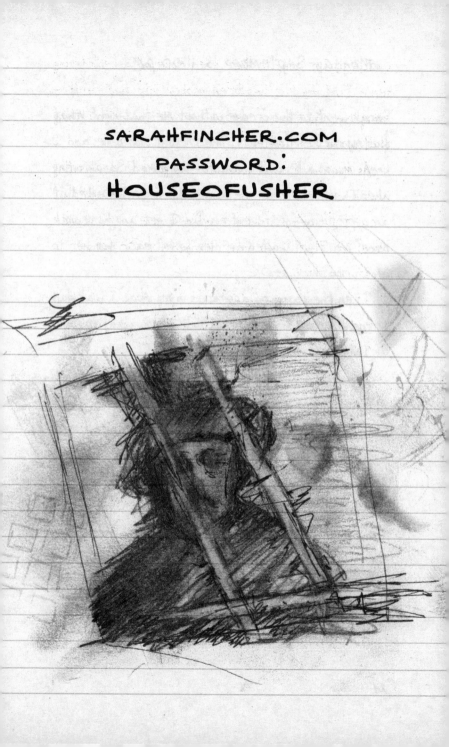

SARAHFINCHER.COM
PASSWORD:
HOUSEOFUSHER

Sarah went to the dredge without me that night. What was my excuse? <u>Homework</u>. She knew it was a lie, and I knew it was a lie, and instead of being mad, Sarah went ahead without me like she always did when I baulked at an opportunity for adventure. Did I get any homework done? No. I just waited for her to get back, for her to send word she was OK.

Then the password appeared in my inbox. I was glad to know Sarah was safe, but I didn't know what to make of the creepy video she'd sent me.

I watched it about ten times that night. I sat at my desk wondering if it was something she'd concocted to scare the wits out of me. That would have been expected, since I'd refused to go with her into the woods. She was always doing that — hoaxing me into feeling guilty.

The next morning, I walked down to her house with the intent of congratulating her on giving me a good scare. I wanted to know how she'd got the effect of the scary face in the window. But the conversation didn't go as I'd expected.

"You think I made it up?"

She said it like she couldn't believe I'd even think such a thing. Like she hadn't done it to me a million times before.

I thought it was still part of the act.

"Don't get me wrong," I said. "It's some of your best work. You really scared me with those gear sounds and — what was that — a man at the window? You must have had help from someone. Who helped you?"

She shook her head. I can remember it so clearly.

"All I did was walk into the woods with my camera. No one helped me do anything."

"You're serious?"

There had been a long pause, followed by a familiar look of determination.

"If you don't believe me, let's go back tonight and you can see for yourself."

If this were a video, not a journal, I'd have to stop. I'd have to rewind. I'd have to play that line again.

"If you don't believe me, let's go back tonight and you can see for yourself."

And again.

"If you don't believe me, let's go back tonight and you can see for yourself."

I didn't know what it would lead to. How could I have?

She didn't even ask. It wasn't, "Do you want to go back tonight and see for yourself?"

No, she was smarter than that.

She didn't give me a chance to say no.

"If you don't believe me, let's go back tonight and you can see for yourself."

We watched the video twice more on her laptop, and both times a chill ran up my spine. It seemed real, and usually when I called Sarah's bluff, she admitted it. Besides, I asked myself, how could she have created something so elaborate and so real? Even for someone with Sarah's editing skill, it seemed impossible.

I believed her.

"Tonight at midnight," she said. "Meet me at the trailhead and we'll go together."

"You're sure about this?"

"Are you kidding? This town is mind-numbingly dull. We're going to die of boredom if we're not careful. Finally, something interesting is happening. Imagine what a great story this will make! All this stuff we're digging up, and now this weird — I don't know what to call it — this phantom at the dredge. It's not a question of whether we want to go back or not. We <u>have to</u> go back."

This was Sarah at her most persuasive. She said it with such urgency — no doubt because it involved her filming, the main thing that took the edge off her boredom.

I have a theory about this. I think what I do is safer than what Sarah does. I can write about whatever I want — monsters, ghosts, arms falling off, people buried alive — and it doesn't matter what I write because it all comes from the safety of my own imagination. But filming requires that there be something to film, and that has a way of leading into real danger.

It certainly did for us.

I really need to sleep now.

Tuesday, September 14, 1:25 a.m.

...but I can't sleep.

It's not the disturbing sound of rusted gears set in motion (though I keep hearing them) or the moving shadows in the upper room of the dredge (I have decided that I <u>hate</u> shadows). What scares me the most is listening to Sarah. I can hear the fear in Sarah's voice. Up until I saw that video I'd never heard her sound like that before.

She just doesn't get scared. When she purchased her first video camera, Sarah interviewed a drifter walking through town. This was a terrible idea. The man was not well-dressed, to say the very least. All of his possessions were tied to his back in black plastic bin bags and he carried a sign that read <u>Los Angeles, if you please</u>.

Sarah talks to strangers all the time without thinking twice about it. She peers into parked cars, eavesdrops in the café, and occasionally tries to sneak into the bar (for lively conversation, not drinks).

When we were eleven, Sarah convinced me we could climb up a steep ravine to the very top. She was right — we made it — but we couldn't get back down without the help of a park ranger, her father, my father, and half the volunteer fire department (three lumberjacks and a retired police officer). This event preceded my earliest memory of stern fatherly advice: <u>Find some other friends.</u> <u>Try out for football if you want, but stop spending so much</u> <u>time with Sarah. She'll only get you into trouble.</u>

There was the hitch-hiking incident, in which Sarah convinced me we needed to visit the metropolis a hundred kilometres away so that we could "observe city dwellers in their native environment". When night approached and we couldn't find a ride back home, we were forced to call my dad. A second warning was offered on the long ride home. <u>You two had better stop acting like idiots. It's</u> <u>only a matter of time before one of you gets hurt.</u>

There was very little else said.

And then, only a month ago, we were caught trying to break into the library on a Thursday night. It was supposed to be closed and we had hoped to find more old newspapers, but we found Gladys Morgan instead. She was sitting in the dark with a shotgun pointed at the door, reading The Sound and the Fury (one of the dullest books ever written). We were very lucky she recognized us. Otherwise she would have filled us so full of buckshot we'd never set foot in a restaurant again without someone mistaking us for Swiss cheese (her words, not mine). She also told us we were dumber than two bags full of rocks. Then she called our parents.

As you can probably imagine, our two sets of parents have long preferred the idea of us staying as far away from each other as possible. It is this long history of trouble that made them respond so forcefully when something really bad finally did happen.

It's why, if they have their way, Sarah and I will never see each other again.

Tuesday, September 14, 2:00 a.m.

I have just made the mistake of checking my email. This is a bad idea in the middle of the night. I should know better. But there was nothing when I checked for messages earlier, not even a measly welcome home. All day I've been wondering if my parents found something and deleted it. It's hard to tell how closely they're monitoring everything.

But now something's slipped through. And I'll admit — I debated whether or not to open it. Because I knew — the moment Sarah and I were in contact, it would start all over again.

Still, how could I resist? I'd never been able to before.

"Learn from your mistakes," part of me was saying.

"They weren't mistakes," another part of me was saying.

And, of course, curiosity won. Or maybe it was friendship that won.

I opened her email.

Ryan,

I'm so sorry about what happened. At least you're home again – that makes me feel a little better. I've hardly left my room. I know they've said we can't see each other because of what happened. I know I'm not supposed to contact you. But it's important that you see this. Please, just drop whatever it is you're doing and watch.

Sarah.

I loved that – <u>just drop whatever it is you're doing</u>. Such a Sarah thing to say. Like I hadn't spent the past two weeks glued to a hospital mattress, wondering when the pain was going to go away.

There was a password attached to the bottom of the email. <u>theraven</u>.

I have to say, I don't appreciate her passwords. It's like she's trying to make things even scarier than they already are. Things are creepy enough without bringing Edgar Allan Poe back from the dead. She knew I'd find her message in the middle of the night while my parents were asleep and every shadow looked like something out to get me.

> Once upon a midnight dreary, while I pondered weak and weary,
> Over many a quaint and curious volume of forgotten lore,
> While I nodded, nearly napping, suddenly there came a tapping,
> As of some one gently rapping, rapping at my chamber door.

Does she even know about this *poem* or is she just pulling these passwords out of thin air?

Something happened fifteen nights ago that has changed everything. I'm sure what Sarah wants me to watch has something to do with that night. It's why I'm writing this down, because my lingering fear has turned to constant alarm these past weeks. I have a dreadful feeling someone is watching me all the time, that someone or something will open the creaking door to my room in the cold night and do away with me. I want there to be some kind of record.

If I wondered whether or not I should open the email, now there's no question in my mind.

Once you're in, you're in.

Once you're caught, you're caught.

I have to watch what she sent. I have to watch it right now.

Tuesday, September 14, 9:00 a.m.

Last night I sort of freaked out. After I watched the video I think I had the second moment of real terror in my life.

The first was having it happen to me.

The second was seeing it.

What was Sarah thinking, sending this to me? I've been scared before — actually, let's be honest, I'm scared most of the time. There's a blind man who sits outside the Rainbow Bar and when I walk by he follows my every move with a clouded white eye — that scares me. At home I hear creaking stairs at night when it should be quiet, and I call out but no one answers. That scares me. The thing living under my bed, Gladys and her shotgun, the woods at night. It all scares me, and it's all like clothes in a dryer that just keep rolling around in my head from one day to the next.

But watching that video last night was different. I couldn't even write. I turned on as many lights as I could reach. I turned on the radio and listened to the church channel until a man started talking about spiritual warfare, which sharpened my fear even more.

The reason the video terrified me was because it made me remember that night. Since it happened, I've had only a fragmented memory, little bits and pieces. But now I remember something more about that night. I remember what I saw that made me fall. It was there in the camera lens at the end.

It was watching me.

It's always watching me.

Tuesday, September 14, 10:15 a.m.

I remember waking up in the hospital. What it was like.

One moment I was falling. Then I saw Sarah's face hovering in the dim light but couldn't hear what she was trying to say. It felt like the bones in my leg had exploded.

Then I was out. When I opened my eyes I actually expected to see the ceiling of my room and smell my dad's coffee brewing downstairs. My head lolled to one side and there sat my parents, glassy-eyed from sleeplessness.

I remember asking, "What's going on?" and my mom jumping up and saying, "Ryan! Go get the nurse, Paul — go on!"

My dad smiled at me, opened the door, and ran from the room. I heard the muffled sound of him yelling for a nurse outside the door. Mom leaned over the bed rail and held my hand.

"Where are we?" I asked.

"You had an accident, but you're awake now — you're awake and you're going to be just fine."

"How long have I been asleep?"

"The nurse — she'll bring the doctor, he'll want to talk

to you. Just stay awake. No more sleeping until your dad comes back with the nurse. OK?"

She squeezed my hand pretty hard, as if it might help keep me from drifting off.

At that point, I didn't have any memory of what had happened to me. There were little bits and pieces, but nothing concrete.

When the doctor came in, I asked if I could use the bathroom and he told me that if I wanted to I could just go ahead and pee. Certain embarrassing arrangements had been made when I was admitted.

"How long have I been asleep?"

"According to your chart you were nonresponsive when they found you at 12:45 a.m. So you've been asleep — or, more accurately, you've been in an unconscious state — for about fifty-five hours."

"So you're saying I've been in a coma?"

"If you want to be dramatic, then, yes, you've been in a coma. You took a pretty good fall. It's amazing you're alive and well enough to tell about it."

"Why can't I move my leg?"

"Because we've surrounded it with a Big Bertha — a

really big plaster cast. I'm afraid it will be a while before you can walk on it again."

I began to fall asleep in the hospital bed. My mom shook my shoulders and yelled at me and the smell of old bicycle tyres went away. I tried harder to stay awake after that because my head hurt and having my mom shout in my face made it hurt even more.

Eventually they took most of the tubes out of my body (including the one that let me stay in bed to use the bathroom). I took some rides in a wheelchair, and my parents started to talk to me. Talking with them was nice at first, because they were truly happy I was OK. But then I asked about Sarah and they both took deep breaths and got serious on me.

"We don't want you seeing her any more," Dad said.

"But she's my best friend," I protested.

Mom took one look at me and I could tell what she was thinking: <u>What kind of best friend nearly kills you?</u>

"Then you'll have to find a new friend," Dad said. "We're serious this time, Ryan. If you can't stay away from each other, we'll move. I'll transfer to the city and we'll sell the house. We don't want to, but we will."

"What are you saying?"

"We're saying you can't see Sarah any more," said my mother. "You're not to contact her — no email, no phone calls — and she won't be coming around when we go home. Her parents agree with us. It's the best thing for a while."

"The best thing for who?"

"You were out in the woods in the middle of the night, breaking into private property," said my dad. He was talking more than usual and for once I wished he'd shut up. "You nearly fell to your death! I think it's fair to say that keeping her away from you is best for everyone, including you."

"It wasn't her fault this time. It was me — it was my idea."

"All the more reason to keep you two apart." My dad was on a roll. "Both your brains go batty when you're together. There's talk in Skeleton Creek of burning that dredge to the ground. The police spent a whole day down there locking it up tight so no one else tries to get in. That thing is a death trap."

After that, my parents went quiet. Neither of them are talkative folks — no one who lives in Skeleton Creek talks very much. They'd laid down the law about Sarah,

41

and that was that. I had to stay there in the hospital for another ten days. I couldn't get online and my parents wouldn't let me use the phone.

What would they do if they knew Sarah was contacting me? They'd sell the house, that's what they'd do.

But there's something in that dredge. She's recorded it twice now. I can't tell my parents, but who doesn't tell their parents about something like this?

I don't know what I'm going to do.

Tuesday, September 14, 11:00 a.m.

Mom just checked up on me. The computer was safely off.

She has no idea.

Or maybe she does.

I wonder if my mom is sneakier than she looks.

The day after I woke up in the hospital, the police came to my room and asked me a lot of questions. They wanted to know if I was trying to steal anything, who else was involved, why I'd done it, did I remember any details about what happened. I didn't tell them anything they didn't already know or couldn't figure out on their own. I went to the dredge, I fell, I got a serious concussion and shattered my leg. What else was I going to say? That I was looking for a phantom and might have found one? I had a strong feeling if I said anything like that they'd move me out of the hospital and into the psych ward.

As it turns out, my mental health was the very reason why they kept me for so many days. I could have gone home a week earlier, but there was a psychiatrist who kept stopping by. My dad was back at work but my mom

43

was still hanging around. She left the room whenever the psychiatrist came in. She (the psychiatrist) was pretty, in a buttoned-up sort of way. She had red hair and glasses and a notepad. She asked me if I'd been taking any drugs or drinking. She asked what I did with my free time and about Sarah. She wondered if she could read some of my stories, and I politely declined. I didn't want her digging around in my stuff. I was pretty sure it wouldn't look good if she found my paranoid rantings about Skeleton Creek.

When they finally let me go home, I had the distinct feeling I'd barely passed some sort of emotional exam they'd run me through. It felt a little like standardized testing at school, like I'd sort of passed but not really, and anyway, I'd never know for sure how I did because they wouldn't tell me. It was an empty feeling.

OK, I know I'm avoiding something. I'm writing quickly, but I'm also dodging what I really should be writing about. Now I'm back to the present — can I avoid it any longer? If I get it down on paper, it will make it real. But maybe if I write it down, I'll fear it less. This strategy often works for me when I'm scared. Writing the things I'm scared of — especially if I turn them into a story — makes them feel as if they've been relegated to the page and I can allow myself to worry less about them in real life.

So here goes.

There was a presence upstairs with me in the dredge before it walked in front of Sarah's camera lens. I was examining the rusted gears, trying to imagine how they could possibly spring to life. The rust came off on my fingers. (Days later, Mom would ask me about the orange mark on my trousers where I'd wiped the rust off, and I wouldn't have an answer for her. I guess I have one now.)

Just as I wiped my fingers, I turned towards the darkened path of boards that led away from the gears where Old Joe Bush had worked. There was a long, wide belt that ran into the black.

And sitting on the belt was a hand.

It was attached to an arm,

the arm to a body,

and the body was moving towards me.

There was a faint light all around the body as it moved closer to me.

I can see it now.

I am seeing it.

It was a silhouette. All in black, so I couldn't make out a face. But the body was large. Whoever — whatever — this was, it was big and slow. It stepped forward, steadying itself on the wide belt as it came, and it dragged its other leg behind.

I remember now how I realized three things all at once. The first was that I couldn't speak. I don't know if it was some force of darkness that constricted my throat or if it was simply pure terror, but either way, the best I could do was keep breathing. (Even that, I now recall, came with great effort.) The second thing — and this one was worse than the first — was that I found myself trapped. I was backed up against the wooden rail behind the gears, which was a corner section of the dredge that looked out over the bottom level. This thing that was after me had me cornered. The last realization I had — worse than the first two put together — was that all my terrible nightmares had finally come true. In the back of my mind, there had always been this one important fact: None of the monsters I'd imagined over the years had ever really come to get me. But now I saw that it was true – there really was a monster, and it really was going to scare me to death.

When it was close enough to touch me, I saw the shadow of its lips move. It spoke to me from beneath the wide brim of a workman's hat.

"Number forty-two is mine. Stay away from this place. I'm watching you."

And then, all at once, my own voice returned. I screamed, I moved back, and the old wooden rail fell away. I remember now looking up as I fell and seeing that whatever had stood over me was gone. It had vanished. Or had it been there at all?

Sarah's video of the leg walking past, dragging the other behind it, makes me surer than ever that what I saw that night was real. I can't tell anyone but Sarah or they'll put me in the loony bin. I felt like people were watching me before the accident, but now it's much worse. My parents are watching me. I'm certain they'll have everyone else in town watching me. On Friday, Henry will arrive and he'll be watching. Gladys with her shotgun is watching me. The raven is watching at my window.

47

And the thing at the dredge — it has to be watching.

Waiting.

Or maybe it's coming to get me.

Tuesday, September 14, nearly p.m.

My leg feels worse tonight. I think it's the stress. There's a deep pain working its way up my back. Besides going to the bathroom, I haven't got out of bed all day. But I've calmed down. Writing everything out helped. It seems more like a story now. It feels better.

I'm finding that dull, lingering pain is ten times worse when it's accompanied by dull, lingering boredom. If not for my laptop I'm pretty sure my parents would have already found me dead from a hopeless case of endless monotony.

I can imagine it:

"Our little Ryan has died of boredom. We should have looked in on him more. Poor thing."

So the laptop rests nicely on Big Bertha. My mom says the psychiatrist gave her some software that secretly tracks my browser history, emails, IMs, everything. It's nice that my mom told me this, because the software isn't very hard to disable. Adults in general take a lot of comfort in these tools, but a fifteen-year-old who can't get around parental controls on a computer is probably also having trouble tying his shoes. It's just not that hard.

Still, timing is important. I can't be searching for weird stuff or sending emails to Sarah without having at least a few minutes to cover my tracks. It takes time to erase what I've done, and it's too late if I've just sent an email and I hear my mom walking up the stairs.

Not that I've sent Sarah any emails. I still don't know what to say.

It's hard. Maybe too hard.

To kill the boredom, I've been searching online for information about the dredge. Sarah and I have looked before and found almost nothing of interest. We searched for archived stories, blogs by people living in town, information about the Crossbones, *The Skeleton Creek Irregular*, and a lot more. In every case we discovered what felt like tiny shards or fragments of information, just enough to keep us going but nothing really earth-shattering.

I tried all those angles again today with the same meagre results. After three hours of dead ends, I looked back through my notes and my eyes lit on the name of the company that had owned the dredge — New York Gold and Silver. I'd searched that term before, but not very aggressively. I went looking for them again, this time with more tenacity.

New York Gold and Silver has been out of business for over twenty years, but one thing about bankruptcy I've found is that all your records are open for viewing. I found a public file of the company records in a subsection of the City of New York legal archives, and within those files I discovered a file marked NYGS AM Mins. 80-85. I knew NYGS stood for New York Gold and Silver. When I double-clicked on the file, I saw that AM Mins stood for Annual Meeting Minutes and that 80-85 meant 1980-1985.

To categorize this document as boring would be way too kind. This was 127 pages of pure, undistilled drudgery. I skimmed the first 30 pages of PE ratios, cost-benefit analyses, plant closures, equity-to-debt ratios, sub-prime holdings, and a lot of other painfully tedious details of a once-prosperous company. It wasn't until I was half asleep on page 31 that I realized I could search for terms I was interested in rather than read every single word.

And that's when I found something on page 81 and something else on page 111 that made me nervous. I printed them out, and I'm going to tape them in here.

NYGS AM Mins. -- Paragraph 3, page 81.

The #42 asset holding in Skeleton Creek, Oregon, encountered a series of break-ins during the period ending 12-81. Mentioned here due to injuries and subsequent lawsuit brought by local resident Mark Henderson. Claimant asserts he was attacked while searching the #42 dredge on the night of 9-12-81, sustaining injuries to the head and neck, including a major concussion. Lawsuit settled out of court on 11-14-81. Legal department cited private property status in early, low six-figure settlement. No information from local authorities is available on a possible suspect in the attack or if such a suspect exists. #42 asset has been more adequately secured. Consider demolition or removal.

NYGS AM Mins. -- Paragraph 1, page 111.

The #42 asset holding in Skeleton Creek, Oregon, was entered by a private citizen during the period ending 12-84. Three juveniles claim to have visited the dredge repeatedly between 6-84 and 9-84. Court file indicates breaking and entering, destruction of private property, theft of tools, vandalism. One of the three juveniles, Jody Carlisle, claims the three were told not to return by someone they heard but could not see. Legal department strongly advises removal or destruction of asset #42. Approved. Demolition of asset #42 scheduled for 4-11-85.

In the spring of 1985, New York Gold and Silver was served with environmental lawsuits from Oregon, Washington, Alaska, Montana and Idaho. I guess they were too busy fending off enemies to take action on their agreement to demolish #42. By June of 1985, the company was dissolved in a sea of debt and legal disputes. Things like the dredge in Skeleton Creek were forgotten as lawyers moved on to higher-profile cases. There was no money to be made suing a dead company.

It's almost nine o'clock now. Mom and Dad will be in to say good night and check up on me. They'll want to check my computer.

I know what I have to do.

Sarah,

This is going to be really quick – I have to cover my tracks before my mom checks in. I did some digging and found the minutes from some New York Gold and Silver meetings in the 80s. I'm copying you on two paragraphs I found (see below). We're not the first ones to see something weird at the dredge. Every time someone gets close, they get hurt or scared off. Don't go back there. Let's just wait until my parents send me back to school so we can talk without having to be so secretive. That's what – maybe a month? We can figure things out when they can't stop us from seeing each other in the halls.

Another thing – New York Gold and Silver called the dredge the "#42 asset". That night, when you recorded the accident, I heard something. It was a warning, the same as those other kids must have got.

"Number forty-two is mine. Stay away from this place. I'm watching you."

And I think I saw him – I think I saw Old Joe Bush. Either that or I'm going crazy.

God, I wish I wasn't writing this as the sun goes down. Write me back – let me know you're okay – but don't do it until tomorrow morning. I'll read and delete.

Don't do anything stupid!

Ryan

P.S. Henry arrives Friday – keep a lookout for him.

I pasted the text from the meeting notes under my name and printed out the email (which is what's included above).

I hope Sarah finds my email before her parents do.

One thing I hate about writing in the digital age is that everything disappears eventually. It's like writing letters that evaporate into thin air as they're read. Which is why I keep copies. Paper feels permanent.

Time to clean up the mess before my parents come up the stairs.

Wednesday, September 15, early a.m.

Mom gave me more painkillers last night — the kind where they warn you not to operate heavy equipment after taking them because you get really drowsy. I fell asleep reading the end of *To a God Unknown*. Steinbeck could be creepy when he wanted to be, like when Joseph Wayne lives all alone at the black rock and listens to the sounds of the deep night until it drives him crazy. I need to start reading different books. Maybe I'll try a romance novel or a memoir about someone who enjoyed a really happy life.

The big news:

Sarah just sent me an email, which I have read, printed, and deleted.

Ryan,

I'm glad you wrote to me. I was thinking maybe you wouldn't. I would've been OK with that.

It seems like we're doing better detective work apart than we ever did together. You're not the only one making progress. I also found something. I'll send a video and a password tomorrow morning – delete the passwords after you get them. We need to keep all this secure where no one but you and I can access.

You're not writing any of this down, are you? Your parents might read this stuff while you're sleeping – that's exactly the kind of thing parents do when they think their son is up to something. Just try not to write things down all the time, OK?

I listened to the audio track on the video again, and the camera didn't pick up a voice that night. It must have been so quiet only you could hear it. I heard the tapping (makes no sense) but no voice. The #42 reference – maybe it means what we're dealing with is somehow connected to New York Gold and Silver.

It's chilling . . . don't you think? I mean, chilling in a good way. Something really important is going on and we're going to figure it out. Whatever caused you to fall – that spirit or phantom or whatever it is – we have to get to the bottom of it. If it really is a phantom – a real . . . *ghost* – what are we going to do? I have to get more evidence on tape or no one is going to believe us.

That stuff you sent – about the company from New York – I'm not worried about it. Those other people were trying to get money or thrills. What we're doing is different – we're serious, like investigators. I'm being careful and quiet – don't worry about me. I'm fine. Oh, and I asked evil eye outside the bar about Mark Henderson, that guy who sued for money. He's long gone. He left Skeleton Creek right after they gave him the money (figures). The kids weren't named, so I think that's a dead end. I guess we could ask Shotgun Gladys. She makes me nervous.

Check back early tomorrow morning, around 5:30 a.m., before your parents wake up. Make sure to get rid of this stuff – my parents put something on my computer to monitor my activity (I disabled it) – did you check your computer? Some of this new stuff is harder to get around.

How's the leg?

Don't write things down.

XO
— Sarah

P.S. The autumn wilderness ranger arrived last night. He's here from Missoula, probably until everything is snowed in. I might interview him like the ones before. Not sure.

I'd never ask Sarah to stop making movies, so she really shouldn't expect me to stop writing. She knows I can't stop. But she makes a good point. If my parents are sneaking around in here after I'm asleep, looking for my journals, I need to make sure they don't find them. I've been putting this one between my mattress and the headboard so I can pull it out and write in it whenever

I want to. I think I'd catch them if they tried to take it while I slept. Wouldn't I?

Oh, man, this reminds me of *The Tell-Tale Heart*. Only six pages, but every one of them seriously spine-chilling. I can imagine my dad quietly entering my room in the dark. He's moving so slowly it takes him an hour to get to my bed — just like the madman in that story. I hear something and sit up, but it's pitch-black and I'm afraid to turn on the light, so I don't see him standing there. I sit upright for a long time and I know someone is in the room even though I can't see them. I'm terrified. And then <u>bang</u>! — he takes my journal and escapes.

Perfect. Now I have one more thing to worry about tonight.

<u>Investigating</u> is often how Sarah gets herself and me into trouble, so I'm worried that she used the word. And her email has that blind confidence she gets sometimes, like she's wearing glasses that only let her see half a metre in front of her own face, nothing to the sides or the back or way out front — just that precious half a metre telling her to charge ahead.

I wonder what she's sending me. It's unbearable having to wait.

Thursday, September 16, early morning

Last night, after dinner, my parents moved me out to the porch so I could get some fresh air. It's getting chilly in the early evening already, but I like that about living in the mountains. The clean air is even crisper when it's chilled. I was exhausted when I finally got back to my room. I fell right to sleep (no doubt the fresh air helped). I got the video and the link from Sarah.

Ryan,

Don't write this down and make sure you delete it and check your tracks. This is SO freaky – we need to talk about it. How? How can we get around your parents?

I'm interviewing the new park ranger with my hidden camera today. Something's not right about him. I saw him at the shops and he wouldn't make eye contact with me. Can't put my finger on it – he's definitely off, like he's trying to hide something. I don't think he knows about what happened at the dredge – or maybe he does. It's on forest service land. Maybe someone told him.

Email me after you watch if you can – my parents are in the house– gotta go.

Sarah

SARAHFINCHER.COM
PASSWORD:
PITANDPENDULUM

Thursday, September 16, morning

So Sarah thinks my ghost — or whatever it was — was there the first night she went to the dredge. And the dragging leg — that would point to Old Joe Bush, wouldn't it?

It's good that Sarah doesn't think I'm insane.

But that might be because she's insane, too.

Either way, she's good company.

I'm supposed to be the paranoid one. But what is she doing? Driving by my house to make sure I'm OK. Checking the doorway ten times a second to make sure nobody catches her. Asking me not to write anything down.

What's going on?

That might be the worst thing about being trapped in here: I have no idea what's going on outside this room.

I wish I could remember more. I don't think I have amnesia... or do I? I remember my name, my age, my address and my phone number. When my mom comes into my room wearing the chilli-pepper apron I gave her when I was in the eighth grade, I recognize her.

I remember, at the age of ten, holding a cold

marshmallow milkshake in one hand while riding my ten-speed down a hill. A dog started chasing me and I squeezed the front brake. After I flipped over the handlebars and landed on my back, I sat up and saw that the dog had lost interest in trying to kill me. He was licking my milkshake off the hot pavement.

You see there? I remember every detail. I remember even more than that.

I remember when I limped home with skinned knees and elbows. My shirt was all dirty. Mom wasn't home, so it was a rare moment in which Dad was my lone hope of sympathy. Mom would have babied me, but I recall feeling as if I'd better not be crying when I reached the porch. I knew he wouldn't like it if I was all upset.

When he saw me, Dad sat me on his lap and touched my stinging knees with a cold dishrag from the kitchen sink.

"Mom's not going to like finding blood all over her good rag," I pointed out.

"Don't worry about your mother. I'll cover for you."

That made me smile, even though I was still concerned. "What will you say?"

"Bloody nose. I'll tell her I got in a fight. I'll say someone punched me."

"She's not going to believe you."

"Cutting vegetables?"

"You only cook pancakes."

"You worry too much."

It was a pleasant moment with my dad, like — I don't know — intimate, I guess. It didn't happen very often. He pushed his T-shirt up with a finger and scratched his bare shoulder. I caught sight of a little mark he had.

"What's that?" I asked.

"Tattoo. From a long time ago. You've seen it before."

"Can I see it again?"

He hesitated. I'd only ever seen the tattoo about three times in my whole life. It was small, about the size of a nickel. He called it his little birdie.

"It doesn't look like a bird."

"It's not a bird. I just call it that."

"What is it then?"

"It's nothing."

He pulled his sleeve back down and set me on the porch. The intimate moment had passed. I remember thinking I'd done something wrong.

So it seems I remember a lot of things — even long strings of things that happened years ago. I just don't recall all the details of the night when I fell. I guess that makes it a blackout, or in my case, a grey-out, since things keep creeping back that I don't necessarily want to remember.

I'm not surprised by what Sarah's saying in the video, about the sound being there both nights. It was like I've already seen and heard this information through a dirty window, and now the window has been cleaned. Things I already knew have become a little clearer, that's all.

But I also think there's something else. When Mom goes to work, I'll be free to watch it again. I'll listen more carefully this time.

Thursday, September 16, 11:00 a.m.

I've watched it now a dozen times. No, more than a dozen. And, yes, I might have discovered something. Not just in the visuals. But the sounds. Especially the sounds — over and over and over again with those sounds. The best way I can describe it is that listening to those sounds again and again is like feeling my memory come unstuck from skipping on an old record. The sound of the leg being <u>dragged</u> — <u>dragged</u> — <u>dragged</u> — and then <u>ping!</u> Something clicked forward in my memory. Something that wasn't there before.

I remember it was dark and I wanted to go home. I was looking at the rusted-over gears, trying to imagine how they could have moved. The torch felt clammy in my hand when I pointed it to a thick wooden beam that stood behind the machinery. Leaning over the biggest of the many gears, I peered down on to the hidden floorboards below. There was a little round mark, about the size of a nickel. I'd seen that mark before.

The record started skipping again.

It's a birdie, it's a birdie, it's a birdie.

After that I saw Old Joe Bush sloshing towards me in his wet boots, dragging his busted leg behind.

What does it all mean?

Sarah,

Your message seems to have nudged my memory. I remember something else from that night that I didn't before. There was a mark or a symbol – I'm not certain what it was – but I saw something carved into one of the wood planks where I stood. It was hidden behind the machinery on the floor. I've drawn a picture and scanned it in so you can see it.

The carving looked like this:

Now, don't get too hysterical, because I have no idea what it means yet, but I'm pretty sure my dad has a tattoo with the same mark. It's the same size and it looks kind of like a bird or an eyeball with some extra junk sticking out.

I'm going to talk with my dad. Don't worry – not about what I saw, not yet at least. I'm just going to ask him about Old

Joe Bush and the dredge and see if he tells me anything. My dad could be connected to the dredge somehow – which is really freaking me out – but I don't want to assume anything.

It's also possible I'm imagining what I think I saw. Don't tell anyone this, OK? But sometimes it feels like my mind is playing tricks on me. I was thinking about the birdie, about an old memory I had, then I watched the video like a dozen times in a row and suddenly I remembered seeing the same thing on the dredge that night. Which memory came first? Are they both real or is one of them imagined? I spend a lot of time thinking about things like this. <u>Too</u> much time.

Listen, Sarah, I don't think I'm going to make it unless I turn this into a story. I'm going to crack under all the pressure. I can feel it. So it's a story, right? I'll call it "The Ghost of Old Joe Bush" – that's what it is – a phantom killed by metal and machines on the dredge. I have to give it a name and write it down so it won't scare me so much.

There's a phantom that carries a hammer in one hand and a lantern in the other. Where did the phantom come from? Why is it pounding on the machinery with the hammer? One of its legs is covered in blood and the blood has left a trail. I could follow the trail if I wanted to. It would lead to the bottom of a black lake, to a secret someone is trying to hide.

This could be a very spooky tale if I really put my mind to it. You think?

I'm calling my dad up here to talk with him and then I'm going to write down everything he says. Maybe he'll tell me something because I'm injured. Sometimes he's sympathetic when I'm hurt. I'll have to ask the right questions.

I have a feeling my parents are paying close attention, even more than when I arrived. They keep warning me not to contact you. Don't get in touch with me very often. Only when you have to. Let's just take it slow.

Be careful! — Ryan

P.S. I'm feeling a little better today. I think I'm going to take on the stairs by myself tomorrow and sit outside. The air is starting to catch that chill I like so much in the late afternoon.

Thursday, September 16, 6:00 p.m.

I talked to my dad.

I'll try to get it all down here.

This is just like I heard it. I swear.

I can remember what we said because I knew I'd have to remember it. It was almost like I recorded the conversation so I could write it down after.

I started off by asking him, "Do you remember when I crashed my bike and you cleaned me up?"

He looked at me a little strangely — this wasn't what he was expecting me to say. But he went along with it.

"I remember," he said. "Your mother found the dishrag in the laundry. She asked if I'd killed a gopher."

"You never told me that."

He shrugged. "How's the leg?" he asked.

"It's stiff until afternoon. Then it warms up and it's not so bad."

"Henry gets in tomorrow morning. We'll bring you outside and you can get some fresh air on the porch. You can watch me skewer him at cribbage. How'd that be?"

I nodded so he knew I thought it was a fine idea.

Then I just went right out and asked, "Did you ever meet Old Joe Bush?"

He paused, sitting at the foot of the bed as he looked at my cast. He got up and left the room. I was sure I'd completely blown it. But when he returned, there was a picture in his hand. He handed it to me.

"That's Old Joe Bush right there."

It was a picture of a man standing before the gears on the dredge, the same gears I had stood in front of on the night of the accident. The gears weren't rusted. They were black and greasy. The man wore work gloves and overalls and glasses. He was a big man, not the slightest bit photogenic. He had the dazed look of someone who had been bothered and wanted to be left alone. Had he been caught in the middle of something important?

"He worked on the dredge, right?" I asked.

My dad nodded almost imperceptibly. "He got careless."

"You mean he got killed?"

He pointed to the picture.

"Those gears pulled him right through and spat him down into the water. They say he drowned because every pocket he had was full of stolen gold. Old Joe Bush sank like his feet were in concrete, right to the bottom."

There was a long silence. My dad walked to the window and looked out, then back at me. And then I felt the sting of why he was talking to me.

"Keep that picture. Let it be a warning. Old Joe Bush got pulled into those gears because he wasn't careful. You nearly died doing something careless yourself. Don't let it happen again."

Even though his message was clear, I figured I might as well ask him something he would probably think was stupid. With my father, moments like this — of true conversation — were pretty few and far between.

"Did Joe Bush ever... come back?" I asked.

From the look in his eye, I could see I was going to get an answer. My dad likes a good story, though I've never known him to write one down. He can tell one if one is needed. He likes the idea of myths and spirits. I think it's part of why I write the things I do. We're both storytellers in our own way and I didn't fall too far from the tree.

"There's a legend that used to be told by some of the last guys who worked on that dredge," he said. "They never talked about it openly, only among themselves. But word gets out."

My dad itched his shoulder where the birdie lay hidden under his shirt.

"They said they could hear Old Joe Bush walking around at night, dragging that cursed leg of his. They could hear him rapping on the metal beams with that big wrench he used to carry around to work on the gears. Biggest wrench anyone ever saw. Tap. Tap. Tap. They'd hear it. Then it would stop. Something would fall mysteriously into the water — something important, like a special tool or a box of parts — but no one was going down into the black to find what went missing. They said Old Joe Bush had wet boots, like he'd crawled up out of the water beneath the dredge where he drowned and came back to claim what was his. Only he couldn't find it."

"Claim what?"

"Why, all the missing gold, of course. What else would he be looking for?"

My dad laughed and said it was only a tall tale. Then he headed for the door.

"Have you talked to Sarah?" he asked, and this time I was surprised by the suddenness of the question.

"No, sir," I said. Technically, this was true. We hadn't actually _talked_. But still I was nervous— my dad had figured me out on lesser lies.

"Let's keep it that way," he said.

And then he was gone.

Thursday, September 16, 9:00 p.m.

Henry arrives tomorrow morning from New York. He hasn't visited since last summer, so I'm very interested to talk to him. When Henry visits, he stays in the guest room downstairs. He and my dad are sort of like best friends, I guess. They fly-fish, hike, play cards and laugh a lot. My dad doesn't usually laugh that much, so it's very noticeable when Henry is around.

I like Henry because, for starters, he's talkative. It can be difficult to make him shut up, if you want to know the truth. I think it has something to do with the fact that everyone else is pretty quiet around here and he's used to more noise in the city. Maybe the sound of his own voice is like the droning background noise he's accustomed to.

Henry wears rainbow-coloured braces and a crisp white shirt wherever he goes, so you can see the good time coming from a long way off. He has muttonchops — and I don't mean for dinner — really wide. Like, Elvis in the 70s sideburns.

He has a reputation for throwing the most outrageous poker parties in Skeleton Creek during his visits. Playing cards with Henry is a little different to cards with normal people, because there's always an unknown array of punishments for losing hands. You might be forced to wear oven gloves and keep playing. Or you could end up in a full-body wet suit, snorkel and an underwater mask. And there are the ridiculous wigs, crank calls to wives and girlfriends, blocks of ice that need sitting on, and helium balloons to be inhaled with preposterous scripts to be read in chipmunk voices. A little bit of money changes hands, but mostly everyone hangs around and laughs really, really hard. Even my dad.

Henry's past in Skeleton Creek is complicated. A long time ago, when the dredge was still tearing up the woods, Henry used to visit more often. That's because he was employed by New York Gold and Silver. He was in charge of what I now know were assets number 42, 43 and 44, all dredges scattered around the western states. That meant constant visits in order to assess progress, hire and fire workers, map the movements of the dredges, package and ship the gold, and basically oversee the operation of not one but three dredges. He was young then, a graduate of Georgetown University, looking to make his mark in the world. He's changed a lot over the years.

I'm hoping he can help me.

Henry was born and raised in the big city, but I think there was something about Skeleton Creek that affected him from the very beginning. It probably happens to a lot of people from New York. They visit Yellowstone Park or Montana or Sun Valley and when they go back home they realize that skyscrapers are not the same as mountains, a hundred taxis are not the same as a hundred cows and the subway doesn't ride like a horse.

I also think Henry feels guilty about working for a company that tore up the land, took all the riches, and left Skeleton Creek high and dry. People seem to like him around here — especially my dad — and there don't seem to be any hard feelings. I think that's because Henry genuinely loves Skeleton Creek and hates what happened to it. Maybe he's doing penance for the work he did in his twenties, back when he didn't know any better. He keeps coming back year after year, burning up all his holiday time on a dead-end town full of dead-end people. I guess that counts for something.

This visit will be much more interesting than Henry's past visits. He stays every autumn for two or three weeks depending on how much holiday time he has saved up. He comes for the September fishing, for the poker, for the friendships. But this is the first autumn when his arrival coincides with my great interest in the dredge. In the past I've spent all my time asking him either about New York or what punishments he has planned for poker night. I haven't asked too many questions about the dredge, at least in part because my dad has always acted like it was a bad idea whenever I brought it up.

But this time I'm going to get Henry alone and really grill him.

Thursday, September 16, 10:00 p.m.

Sarah has sent me another video already. Two in one day. She's getting way too careless. I saw the email, but I'm going to wait another hour or two before watching the video so my parents are asleep. The videos are hard enough to watch without the added pressure of wondering whether or not my mom or dad are going to knock on my door. I can't erase my tracks that quickly.

I wonder what she wants.

Thursday, September 16, 11:12 p.m.

That was close. I barely hid my journal in time. If I'd been in the middle of a sentence, I probably would've been caught.

My parents are getting too curious. They're in my room all the time, asking a lot of questions. They keep pestering me about Sarah. Have I talked to her? Have I seen her? Did I know she drove by in the middle of the night?

They came in together right after I finished my last entry.

Dad said, "Don't think just because Henry is coming we're not going to be watching you as closely. We want you out of this bed tomorrow, downstairs or on the porch."

Mom said, "You need to start getting more fresh air. Let's do that tomorrow, OK?"

Then Dad said, "Let's have a look at that computer."

It's just dumb luck Sarah hadn't sent me something in the previous hour, and that I'd already scribbled down the password from her previous email (which I'd already deleted). They'd have seen it before I did, before I could erase it. My nerves are shot and I'm really tired.

I keep having to stay up late and get up early so I can work with Sarah without getting caught. I'm not sure how much longer I want to do this.

But I can't ignore the latest password.

Amontillado

From *The Cask of Amontillado* – a terrible story about deception and revenge. I'm certain she's never read it. Fortunado tricked and chained, the slow building of a wall to trap him underground. It's a really awful story, not one of my favourites. Maybe if I told her the story, she'd stop picking such ghastly passwords.

Tomorrow might get complicated. I better watch tonight, even though I can barely keep my eyes open.

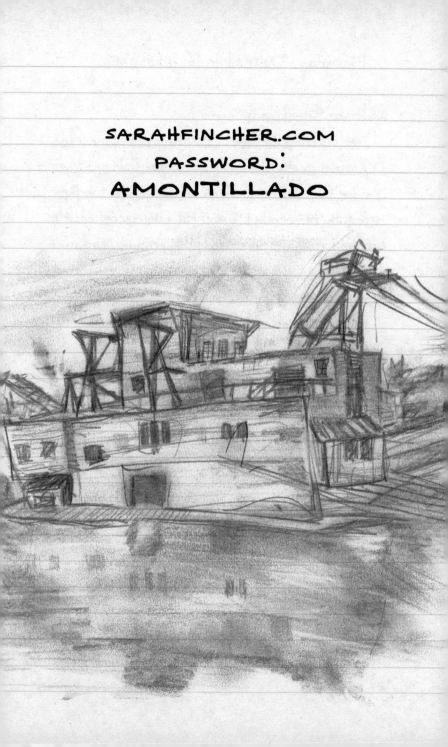

SARAHFINCHER.COM
PASSWORD:
AMONTILLADO

Thursday, September 16, 11:58 p.m.

What was it that Sarah said?

I'm starting to think everything is connected. The secret society, the dredge, New York Gold and Silver, Old Joe Bush — I think it's all somehow linked together.

But that's not all. It's not just some secret society, New York Gold and Silver, and Old Joe Bush. It's Sarah. And me.

And now this new wilderness ranger.

Why did he ask Sarah if we saw anyone at the dredge?

What does he know?

Which is the same thing as asking:

What don't we know?

I have to try to get some sleep.

If I can

Friday, September 17, 7:10 a.m.

I have this very weird feeling that someone came into my room last night. I woke up but I was too afraid to look around. Plus, it was dark. I couldn't shake the feeling. And then I started wondering if I'd deleted the history after I watched the last video. I reached under my pillow and felt for my journal. It was there. It doesn't seem like it was moved.

It's crazy how paranoid I am.

I've been lying in bed for an hour staring at the picture my dad left me and replaying his warning in my mind.

<u>Old Joe Bush got pulled into those gears because he wasn't careful. You nearly died doing something careless yourself. Don't let it happen again.</u>

After sixty-one minutes of contemplation, I've determined that what my father asked of me was stupid. Carelessness may not be a virtue, but it's unavoidable, especially for someone my age. And besides, super-careful people are really boring. I know a girl at school who won't drink out of the water fountain. She won't eat food from the cafeteria. She has a note for gym class that allows her to sit out whenever we do something she feels is too dangerous. She barely has a pulse.

Old Joe Bush doesn't look like the careless type. If I had to say what he looks like in his picture, I'd say . . . well, I guess I'd say he looks single-minded. Probably he was pushed. Foul play, that's what killed Old Joe Bush, not carelessness.

It was really late when I watched Sarah's video last night. I dreamt about it, so when I woke up I wasn't sure if I'd watched it at all. In my dream, Daryl Bonner the ranger and Gladys the librarian were walking in the woods. Gladys had her shotgun and then Old Joe Bush came out of the bushes dragging his leg and said, "Number forty-two is mine. Stay away from this place. I'm watching you." Gladys fired buckshot into the air, and Old Joe Bush tried to run away, dragging his leg down the path towards the dredge. Gladys laughed and laughed, but Daryl Bonner went on ahead and helped Old Joe Bush step down into the black pond and disappear under the water. In my dream, the pond looked like a tar pit.

The thing about dreams is that they sometimes mean something. I have dreams all the time, but I get this feeling about certain dreams that makes me think something important is hidden there. This was one of those dreams. The sticky goo of the tar pit hides things. I know it does.

I don't think Gladys is important. I think she's just in there because I'd never gone through a door and found someone pointing a shotgun at me. She's been appearing in a lot of dreams since. She's like wallpaper. She's just there.

But Ranger Bonner — he's new — and he's helping Joe into the water or the tar. Why did I connect the two in my dream? My unconscious mind must see something in the video or the picture that my waking mind doesn't. An hour of looking at the picture my dad gave me isn't helping me see things clearer. I'm going to risk watching Sarah's video again, but this time I'm going to keep the picture handy so I can look at it. It's almost 7:30 and my mom usually comes in between 7:30 and 8:00.

I better hurry.

Thursday, September 16, 10:00 p.m.

No sign of Mom yet, and I've watched the video again. I scanned the picture of Old Joe Bush and sent it to Sarah. Dangerous move. If her parents open her email before she does, they'll suspect I've sent it. Even though I used an account that doesn't have my name on it and I didn't say hardly anything.

This is Joe Bush – familiar?

I didn't put my name at the end. I just attached the photo and sent it.

I think I know why Daryl Bonner and Joe Bush are together in my dream. It's because in real life they look sort of similar. The photo is grainy, but the bone structure, the nose, the forehead – they're similar. _Too_ similar.

What does that even mean?

Friday, September 17, 8:00 a.m.

Mom has been here with my breakfast and gone. It was a miracle she didn't check my computer, because I totally forgot to erase my tracks. It feels like every day I'm a whisper away from losing everything, including my best friend. I totally believe my parents when they say they'll sell the house and move us to the city if they catch me talking to Sarah. If they knew how much we were emailing — all the stuff we were doing — they'd pack the car and have me out of here tonight.

Like Dad said, I have to be careful. I can't be careless when it comes to communicating with Sarah. There's too much at stake.

I've got something weird I want to try — just to see what will happen. It's not the most careful thing in the world, but I can't stop thinking about it.

Here's my plan:

I'll call the ranger station. It's early, so Ranger Bonner probably won't be on the trail yet. When he picks up I'll ask for Joe Bush and see what he says. I wonder what he'll do? What if he has caller ID? Do ranger stations have stuff like that?

I'm risking it. If I get caught, I'll say it was a prank. I'll play up the fact that I'm crazy.

Friday, September 17, 8:10 a.m.

I called Daryl Bonner.
Here's what happened:

Him: "Skeleton Creek Ranger Station."
Me: "Can I speak to Joe Bush?"
Him: "Who is this? Why are you asking for Joe Bush?"
I didn't reply.
Him: "Did Sarah Fincher put you up to this?"
I didn't reply.
Him: "Answer me! Why are you asking about Joe Bush?"

I hung up.
And now I wonder:
Why was he so freaked out?

Friday, September 17, 9:15 a.m.

I have just endured an eventful hour and five minutes. About two minutes after I hung up, the phone rang. I tried to intercept the call myself, but I picked up at the same moment my dad did. He's a notoriously quick grabber of the phone. He hates hearing it ring and ring. I thought he'd already be halfway out the door for work, but I guess he stayed late this morning.

Just my luck.

Dad: "Hello."

Bonner: "This is Daryl Bonner at the ranger station. Did you just call this number?"

Dad: "I did not. My son might have."

Bonner: "Is this the home of the boy who had the accident at the dredge?"

Dad: "Might be."

Bonner: "I think he might be getting bored. He just called here with — I don't know — I guess you'd call it a prank call. He asked for Joe Bush, whoever that is. And the girl involved in that accident — Sarah Fincher — she seems interested in the dredge as well. It might be a good time to keep an especially close eye on them both. The dredge isn't safe — at least that's what the state supervisor told me. No one should be going out there."

Dad: "I'll have a talk with my son."

Bonner: "Thank you."

I hung up right after they did, then listened to my dad coming up the stairs and wondered if my actions qualified as more than careless. I had the feeling they did. Sarah's interview ran through my head, then my call. I felt stupid for having done it. There were dots that could be connected. Sarah, Bonner, me. There was a flurry of activity. Maybe it was enough to get the house on the market.

I already had a fondness for Henry, but when the doorbell rang and my dad went back downstairs I liked Henry ten times more. Our autumn visitor had arrived, and I was spared my dad's wrath. His anger usually boiled over pretty fast. If I could stay out of his crosshairs while he calmed down, the consequences were always less severe. Until he showed up in my room with Henry in tow, I even had a glimmer of hope that my dad had forgotten all about the phone call.

"That's one heckuva cast!"

Those were the first words out of Henry's mouth when he came into my room with my dad. They were both smiling and I breathed a sigh of relief.

Henry went on, "Any chance I could have it when you're done? That thing could be a real hit at the card table."

"They'll have to cut it off. I could only give you the pieces."

"I've got duct tape. It'll be perfect."

Henry had his fishing hat on, edged with flies, and his rainbow braces.

"Your dad tells me he needs to run across town and see the ranger. Mind if I keep you company while he's gone?"

"I'd like that."

My dad asked for his picture of Old Joe Bush, and I gave it to him. He looked at me as if to say, <u>We're not quite through here yet, I'll be back</u>, and then he left me and Henry alone in my room. I <u>so</u> wish I'd never made that phone call. It feels like I've opened a can of worms and they're squirming out all over the place.

Henry chimed in when the sound of our front door closing reached my room.

"Can you get down those stairs?" he asked.

"I think I can. But I always feel better in the afternoon. I think I'll wait a little bit."

"Fair enough. How bored are you?"

"Very."

"I suspected."

"How long are you staying?"

"A week of bliss! Two poker nights, fishing on the river, and your mom's home cooking. You don't appreciate it now, but Cynthia is the queen of comfort food. Old bachelors love comfort food, especially when we're from the city. She's making that baked noodle dish with the crunchy cheese on top tonight. I've been thinking about it for three days."

"You should get married," I joked.

"And give up Yankee games, dirty laundry, and my twelve girlfriends? I don't think I'm ready for that kind of sacrifice."

"You don't have twelve girlfriends."

"Do so."

"Liar."

"Well, I've <u>had</u> twelve girlfriends. It's the same thing."

"I bet all twelve are now married with kids and have long since forgotten the Yankee-loving slob they dated ten years ago."

"You shouldn't talk like that with a cast on your leg. You won't be able to run away when I dump a bucket of cold water on your head."

"You're all talk."

"I'm making your lunch."

Henry smiled and I knew I was in big trouble. I hated not knowing what disgusting thing he might add to a Hot Pocket or swirl into peanut butter before spreading it around. He probably wouldn't do anything, but I'd never know for sure, and it would drive me crazy.

We talked about the accident and about how I couldn't see Sarah any more. The news about Sarah bothered him and he said he would talk to my parents. He liked Sarah and I appreciated it, but I knew somewhere deep down that it didn't matter what Henry said. My parents had already made up their minds.

I had no idea how many more times I'd have Henry to myself. I decided it was time to begin my inquisition, especially since he was in such a friendly mood.

"Hey," I said. "How come you never talk about when you used to work for New York Gold and Silver?"

"It's not my best chapter."

"Why not?"

Henry took off his hat and laughed nervously. Then his smile went away and I felt terrible for asking him.

"Since you're all busted up, I suppose I'll tell you. I made a lot of mistakes back then because I was young and ambitious. I could lie and say I didn't really know what I was doing, but I knew. Skeleton Creek got into my bones, though. It saved me."

"Did you ever meet Joe Bush?"

Henry looked at me a little curiously then, but he still answered. "Why sure I did — lots of times. He was a hard worker. You know he died on the dredge?"

"I do."

"That accident was the beginning of the end. I quit not too long after that. There were a lot of lawsuits flying around. They were asking me to do things I couldn't do."

"Like what?"

"You sure are curious when you're laid up."

"Like what, Henry?"

"They wanted me to lie about things, and that's when I knew for sure I'd been doing something wrong all along."

"Did you ever hear of Old Joe Bush coming back?"

"You mean like a ghost?"

"I guess so."

"Let's just say there are stories floating around — none of them true, mind you — about the ghost of Old Joe Bush. It's all hogwash."

"Can I ask you one more thing?"

"Sure you can."

"Have you ever heard of the Crossbones?"

"Now there's an interesting question!"

"Really?"

"It's especially interesting for an outsider like me. Did you know membership is only allowed if you can prove you were either born here or have a relative that was born here?"

"No. I didn't know that."

"That's the truth — or at least I think it is. I'm pretty sure the Crossbones came into existence back when the dredge was still working."

"Why do you say that?"

"There was talk of a secret group forming. You hear things."

"What did they do?"

"If I knew that, I'd be a member. But as I said, I'm from the outside. A New Yorker, no less! No matter how much I love this place or how many times I come back, I'll never know more than I do right now about the Crossbones. Which isn't much."

I was afraid to ask one last question, but I asked anyway.

"Is my dad a member?"

"If I were a betting man, I'd put good money on it. But the truth is, I have no idea. We talk about a lot, but not about those kinds of things."

Then he left to unpack his things, and I wrote all of this down.

I can't wait to tell Sarah.

But how?

It's riskier with someone else around. I don't think Henry would tell my parents if he caught me emailing — but I can't be sure.

Friday, September 17, 11:00 a.m.

When Dad came back, the steam had gone out of his anger and he didn't say a lot about the call I'd made. He didn't give me back the picture of Joe Bush and I didn't ask for it.

"I know you're bored," he said, "but leave that poor man alone. He's new in town and he's got work to do like the rest of us. Find something productive to do."

Like the <u>rest</u> of us? I don't know what he's talking about. My dad is on vacation for the next week while my mom keeps working at the post office like she always does. Henry and my dad will sleep late, make pancakes and strong coffee, then fish and play cards.

I keep wondering how my dad would feel if someone told him he couldn't see Henry ever again. I'm pretty sure he'd go down fighting.

The two of them are downstairs going through their fly boxes, comparing gear, getting ready to go fishing on the river for the afternoon. Skeleton Creek drains into a bigger creek, and that bigger creek drains into the river, where they'll search out winter-run steelhead (basically a giant trout). The place they're going to is an hour outside of town if my dad is driving the old pickup. He has to baby it or they'd be there in half the time.

When Dad and Henry get back they'll throw together a late lunch and help me down to the porch and we can play cards before Mom gets home.

What did my dad say to Ranger Bonner? He might not have even seen the ranger. Maybe he only said he was going to see Ranger Bonner and actually went to talk with Sarah's parents or, worse, an estate agent. There could be a sign going up in the front yard already.

I despise all estate agents.

Friday, September 17, 11:40 a.m.

They left here fifteen minutes ago and I drifted off to sleep. At first I thought there was a phone ringing in my dream, but it kept ringing, and on the fourth ring I reached out my arm and fumbled for the cordless. I expected it to be Mom checking on me. She has a way of knowing when I'm home alone. She tells me to rest, eat and stay off the Internet.

I clicked on the receiver and answered groggily, hoping she'd hear the fatigue in my voice and go easy on me with the lecturing. When I answered, there was the faintest sound of — what was it? — leaves moving in the trees? Or was it water moving? It had the distinct but indefinable sound of nature. At least that's what I thought before whoever it was hung up on me.

My first thought was that my dad was calling from the stream to make sure I was staying put. But why did he hang up? I looked at the caller ID and didn't recognize the number. It was a 406 area code. Not local.

I dialled the number and waited. One ring. Two rings. Three rings. Voice mail.

"This is Daryl Bonner with the Montana Department

of Fish and Wildlife. I'm currently stationed in Skeleton Creek, Oregon, returning to the Wind River Station on November third. Please leave a message."

Why is Ranger Bonner calling my house and then hanging up? Was he looking for my dad and got me instead?

I shouldn't have called him and asked if Old Joe Bush was there.

What if he thinks I know something I'm not supposed to?

Friday, September 17, 1:20 p.m.

I've spent the last couple of hours scouring the web for anything about Skeleton Creek, the dredge, Old Joe Bush. I'm so frustrated. It's like I've dug up all the bones I'm going to find and they make up only about a tenth of what I'm searching for. The deeper I go, the harder the ground feels. I feel like I've hit a layer of solid rock.

I need to send a warning to Sarah, but I'm afraid to. What if my dad went to her parents and they've taken her computer? I can see them sitting at the kitchen table, hitting refresh every fifteen minutes, waiting for my email to come through. The death email. The email that sends me packing.

I can't risk it.

Friday, September 17, 1:25 p.m.

Obviously Sarah doesn't feel as concerned as I do, because I just got an email from her. I guess that puts to rest my concern about her parents confiscating her laptop. Unless — and this is entirely possible — they're baiting me. What if they sent the email? Or, worse, what if my dad is on Sarah's laptop at her house with her parents sending me emails? It's an underhanded move, but it could happen.

I'd like to think Henry would tip me off. But how could he?

I'm hungry and tired, which sometimes makes me nervous. But seriously — I am so paranoid. It's ridiculous. Maybe I need group therapy. Me, Sarah and Old Joe Bush.

Actually, to be fair, what I got from Sarah wasn't really an email if you consider there were no words in the message, only a string of letters in the subject line and nothing else.

drjekyllandmrhyde

So now she's diverging from Poe into Stevenson. Fair enough.
I sometimes think she's trying to tell me something with
these passwords. Like in this case, is she saying that Daryl
Bonner is Dr Jekyll, and the ghost of Joe Bush is Mr Hyde?
Or is Daryl Bonner both?

Or is my dad both?

I can't believe I just wrote that. I might as well be
Jekyll and Hyde, I keep going back and forth.

I have to get out of this house.

Dad and Henry could come back early. I haven't
covered the tracks of my two hours of searching online.
I haven't deleted Sarah's email or watched the video.
There's a lot to do while I have the house to myself.

I'm getting rid of everything first. Then, if I'm still
safe, I'll watch the video.

SARAHFINCHER.COM
password:
DrJEKYLLANDMRHYDE

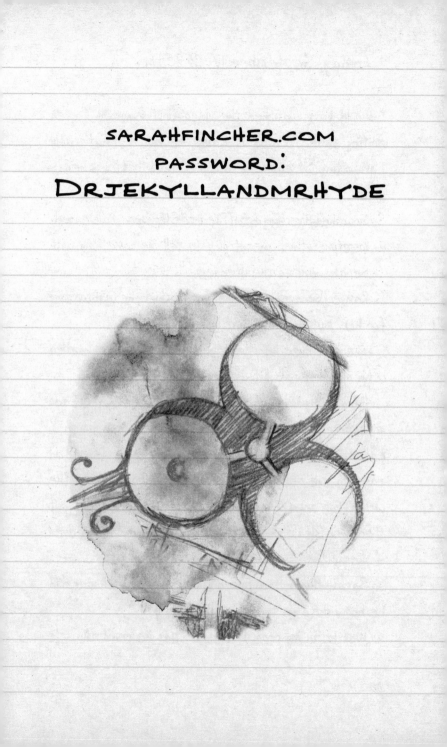

Friday, September 17, 1:52 p.m.

I should have watched the video first! Why am I even writing this? Because it calms me down. That's why I'm writing. It calms me down. I think better when I write.

I can figure this out if I settle down.

Recap:

Sarah went to the dredge.

Ranger Bonner was there. Sarah thinks he was waiting for her. But she could just be overreacting.

She borrowed his phone. She dialled the last number in his incoming calls list.

It was my house. And it was after Dad had already gone over to talk to Bonner. Supposedly. And when I called back? He must have had the ringer silenced in case it went off while he was tailing Sarah through the woods. For once I'm glad there is mobile reception out there — at least she could get a signal and call me, even if she couldn't say anything.

Sarah thinks Dad tipped Bonner off. But how could he know she'd be there?

Was he in my room last night? Has he read this? He

could have sneaked in here just like that crazy nut job in *The Tell-Tale Heart.* I woke up — it felt like someone was in the room, but there was no one. Or at least no one answered in the dark.

If my dad knows, then why isn't he confronting me? Why isn't the house up for sale? Why isn't my mom freaking out? She's not, so that means he hasn't told her.

How many questions is that — fifty? I can't answer any of them for sure. I need more information. I need to narrow this down.

What's the most important question right now?

Dad. What's going on with Dad?

Twenty minutes tops, maybe fifteen. I can't risk sneaking around beyond that. They'll stop fishing when Henry gets hungry. Henry likes to eat. He'll want to knock off early. I bet they'll be here by 2:30, maybe even earlier.

I'm just going to take my journal with me — that's what I'm going to do. I'll keep writing. I'll hobble to my parents' room, right down the hall. I can make that work. I'll go in there. I know where my dad's dresser is. I know he keeps his personal stuff in the top drawer because Mom told me when I was little. She caught me in there and slapped my hand really hard and said I should never search through other people's things without asking. She said it was the same as stealing, which I never really understood.

I'm in the door. My watch says 2:03 but I'm leaving the door open so I can hear it if they come in. Henry will be loud — he'll be talking. I'll be able to get out.

My parents' walk-in wardrobe smells like my mom, not like my dad. I'm having some trouble breathing. I just can't seem to calm down. I remember when she slapped my hand and how it stung. The blood is rushing through my leg and I can feel every part that's broken. It feels like my mom took a broomstick and started beating me with it. Whack! Whack! Whack!

I've got this journal open on the top of the dresser. The lightbulb doesn't make it very bright in here. It's sort of a yellow light. Oh, man, I can't breathe very well. Do I have asthma? I might have asthma, the more I think about it. I've kicked up some dust in here. My leg is killing me. It doesn't like being stood up for too long all at once.

I know it's crazy for me to be writing as I do this. But I have to.

I might not get another chance to do this. And I can't rely on my memory. I have to get everything down.

The drawer is open. There's lots of stuff in here. My grandfather's belt buckle — he's dead now. It's got rhinestones in it. A stack of documents — legal stuff, I think. A cigar box with a little latch on it. Some rings and pens and old watches.

I've opened the cigar box. It's got a row of ten or twelve matching cuff links pushed into a sheet of cardboard. My dad never wears cuff links. There's an old badge, a stack of expired credit cards and licences. There's nothing ominous here. There's no sign of a secret society.

2:12. I have to get out of here.

Why cuff links? I bet they're from their wedding day — maybe it's all the cuff links from all the men in the wedding party. They all look alike, as if they were worn once and never again.

2:13.

I tried to pick up one of the cuff links, and the whole piece of cardboard lifted up out of the cigar box. When I flipped it over, I found a piece of paper taped to the back. I unfolded it and found something there. I can't breathe. I <u>really</u> have to get out of here.

2:15.

They're going to be back any second now. I can feel it. I've shuffled back down the hall to my room, dragging my leg behind me. My computer is scanning the piece of paper while I write. Come on — finish!

2:18.

The scan is done. Time to return the original.

2:20.

They're home! Henry just yelled up the stairs.

"I'm making lunch, champ! I hope you're ready for a surprise!"

I'm standing in front of my dad's dresser with the little yellow light on. I can't move. He'll come up here any second, I know he will. Then what will I do? I should run. I should get out of here. I've closed the drawer but I can't move.

What am I going to do?

He's coming.

Friday, September 17, 2:41 p.m.

I've calmed down now. I'm not shaking so much any more. I can breathe again. My dad went straight to the hallway bathroom on his way to my room. I heard him yell.

"Just going to use the head and I'll stop in and see you. Fishing was good! Better than last year."

I made it out of his room, into the hallway outside the bathroom door. I tucked this journal in the top of my cast and sucked in my breath. The door opened with a whoosh of air.

"Look at you! Up and walking around. You must really want to play some cards."

He looked happy to see me. I felt guilty about that. What was I doing?

"Count me in," I told him. "I'm tired of lying down."

"Looks like you just ran a marathon. How about lunch in bed, then we'll help you to the porch? Deal?"

"Deal."

And so Dad delivered me back to my room, and then Henry brought in a grilled-cheese-and-bacon sandwich with tomato soup. It would be easy to hide all sorts of gross things in creamy red soup or melted orange cheese. But it was late and I was starving. He wouldn't dare trick a kid with a cast. Would he?

Friday, September 17, 2:47 p.m.

Dad and Henry will be up to get me any minute.

I printed out the scan of what I found. I'm sticking it on this page.

It scares me.

THE ALCHEMIST DIAGRAM of 79 for PAUL McCRAY

NUMBER One iS WEARY WHEN
THREE GOES PAST THE TWO
1st day \ next month \ 2:30am

TWICE ROUND THE MOON WITH
SEVEN FINGERARD SAM
7th day \ current month \ 2:00 am

TWELVE tiMES tHE tORtOiSE
WHEN tHREE tURNS tHE HARE
12th day \ current month \ 3:00 am

FIVE MY SING INC MINTREE,
TWELVE TAKES THREE TO DINNER
8th day / next month / 12:30 am

SLeeP You COWARD FooL,
WAKE WHEN BiRDiE tURNS
people are watching \ keep quiet for a time

EIGHT BALL CORNERED,
BISHOP TAKES QUEEN
18th day \ current month \ 4:00 am

A STRaIGHT SHOT TO MARtHA'S
AT TEN PAST THE KNOB
comnavy meeting \ tonight \ 10 past midnight

THE FLOOR AND 7tH.
FOUR PAST THE NINE ·
on DooR NUMBER TWO!
LIBRARY ATTIC.
ENTER THROUGH THE
ALLEY DOOR MARKED 203.

MAN PLAYS FIDDLE
AT NINE IN THE MIDDLE
UJDER STAIRS ON SIX
OPEN THE FLOOR
MARKED 9 ON LOWBHERE
BLACK STAGE THE
SIXTH STAIR DOWN.

Friday, September 17, 7:30 p.m.

There's no two ways about it: Navigating stairs is complicated with a full-leg cast and crutches. Our stairwell is narrow and there are family pictures hanging like clumps of grapes all the way down both sides. I think I would have been fine if I hadn't insisted I could do it alone. Henry and Dad were watching from the bottom of the stairs when I pitched forward somewhere near the middle and lost my balance. Dad met me with outstretched arms, and my face smashed into his grey T-shirt. He smelled like a fisherman.

My hands fanned over about a dozen family pictures in frames on the way down but by some miracle of gravity none of them fell to their deaths. They wobbled back and forth and knocked into one another, but they held. It looked like a big gust of wind had rushed through.

In my defence, the cast is really heavy and... let's see... what's the word I'm searching for? ... <u>Unbending</u>. A cast like Big Bertha makes a person want to bend like never before. I'm <u>dying</u> to bend my leg. It's like a ferocious itch I can't scratch. (Which reminds me: this thing itches like mad, so add that to my list of complaints.)

When I finally made it to the front porch, the floorboards creaked under the weight of my cast. I settled down on a gold, tattered couch with my leg propped up on a wooden stool and breathed in the crisp autumn air.

Our porch is a lot like an outdoor living room. When a piece of furniture is replaced inside the house, the old item finds a home on the porch. After a while — a year, maybe two — the same item moves three more metres and becomes an item in one of Mom's many yard sales. It's a natural progression, a slow but steady march off the property.

I searched the skies for flying Dr Pepper cans or other signs of Sarah, but there was nothing. Henry asked if I wanted to play three-handed cribbage. Not a great game if you ask me. I'm not sure who came up with it, but probably it was three people sitting in a room with one cribbage board and the person sitting out wanted to join in. I played anyway. It was nice to think about something other than haunted dredges and secret societies.

"How much longer?" Henry asked after a little while. He was holding his cards with one hand and tugging slowly on one of his rainbow braces with the other.

"Before what?"

"Before you can walk around without something on your leg?"

"How long, Dad?"

"Seven weeks."

Henry couldn't believe it. "Seven weeks! You'll have to ship the cast to me. I'll leave a box."

"You're nuts," I told him.

"I bet it itches like termites."

"It does."

"You could jam a coat hanger down in there."

Henry is a great card player. He has this maddening way of distracting everyone with all sorts of mindless small talk. He'd never admit it, but I'm sure this is part of his strategy. It's hard to concentrate when someone's talking about having an empty cast shipped to New York. I started thinking about what the box would look like. I wondered what his twelve girlfriends would say when they saw the cast propped up against the wall in his apartment. I started feeling almost positive there were bugs crawling around inside my cast. I begged my dad to go and get me a coat hanger. And all the while I made stupid plays all over the cribbage board.

Eventually I got my coat hanger straightened out and jammed it all the way down to my kneecap. That was an improvement. We basically sat there playing cards for about an hour, talking about nothing in particular — mostly, Henry was trying to throw us off, and was doing a hit-or-miss job. Eventually Mom came home, and after calling hellos, we heard her pounding away on the pipes in the kitchen.

"You should go help her," Henry said.

Henry has a lot of sympathy for my mom. He knows my dad isn't very good about taking on home projects. My dad is plenty capable, but he lacks motivation for certain kinds of tasks.

"You go help her," Dad said.

"What's she doing in there?" Henry asked.

"Trying to unclog the waste disposal," my dad said. "She's under the sink, hitting the pipe with a rolling pin. Believe it or not, it usually works."

"Sounds a little like the old dredge when it was really cranking."

My mom started yelling at the sink, which prompted my dad to set his cards down, sigh deeply, and walk indifferently to her rescue.

There was something about that noise — the sound of banging on metal — that made me think again of the night I'd fallen and smashed my leg. There had been a clanging sound, barely audible, as if someone was hitting metal on metal.

I decided to ask Henry about his comment.

"What sound do you mean?"

Henry leaned back in his chair until it was only on two legs.

"The dredge was incredibly loud. Tonnes of rocks were scooped from the ground and dumped inside. The conveyor belts were edged with thick planks of wood that kept everything from falling out. It was like a long water slide — you've seen those? — but instead of water shooting through, it was boulders. It echoed like mad, which seemed to quadruple the rumbling. Such a horrible sound. A crew of four was required to run the dredge, and they were separated by quite a distance. One was stationed at the gears in front where they watched everything come in. That person greased the machines and pulled the stop-chain if things got jammed up. Another was at the far end, watching the tailings dump out. There was a man at the control booth and one more we called a roamer —

a guy who fixed things on the fly from a running list of problems."

"But the sound — the banging — what sound was that?"

"The workers couldn't hear one another. They couldn't yell that loud. So they used signals. They banged metal wrenches or hammers against the iron girders of the dredge to tell each other things. It was like Morse code, simple but effective in those days."

When Dad returned, the conversation veered quickly away from the dredge. I didn't want him to hear us talking about it, and maybe Henry didn't, either. Instead, we all played cards and talked about the Yankees and the Mariners. After a while, Mom brought the casserole with the crispy cheese top and the last of the late summer bees started swarming around the porch.

Friday, September 17, 9:00 p.m.

I've spent a lot of time away from my bedroom today,
which makes me feel anxious. I feel like the FBI has
scoured my mattress and squeaky box spring, taken pictures,
dusted for fingerprints — all the while with two-way
radios wired to the kitchen so Mom could tell them if
I was on my way and they could jump out the second-
storey window. I know this sounds stupid, but it's how I
feel all the same.

The room appears untouched. Before I left I took
Sarah's advice and found a better hiding place for this
journal. I slid it inside my ninth-grade annual from last
year and put the annual between a whole bunch of other
books. I also taped it shut. It doesn't look to me like they
found it. The seal hasn't been broken.

They'll leave me alone for a while — Henry's got all
their attention — so it's a good time to email Sarah and
tell her about what I found in my dad's dresser.

Friday, September 17, 1:52 p.m.

Too late, she already emailed me. It was a short, bad email. The worst kind.

I'm going back tonight. I have to. Don't worry – I'm fine. I'll contact you tomorrow. Delete this!   S

So I emailed her back.

Sarah,

Have you lost your mind? Don't get anywhere near the dredge right now! People are probably watching. And besides that, I'm digging up all sorts of reasons to stay clear of that thing (as if a phantom isn't reason enough!). I found something in my dad's room. You're amazed I went in there, right? Me too. Trust me, it was insane. I attached a scan of what I found. It feels like dangerous information to have. It will ring a bell from the ads we found in the old newspapers about the Crossbones. I think they're still meeting. I think my dad is one of them. Did I mention that I'm shaking right now? I'm telling you, Sarah, stay away from the dredge. Don't go back there tonight. We're getting too close.

123

I found out something else about the sounds I heard that night – I have to get off-line but I'll send it later. I'm still figuring it out.

Stay put!!

Ryan

Friday, September 17, 9:40 p.m.

Is it normal to get into the habit of erasing everything?
I get the distinct feeling I'll be doing it for the rest
of my life. I'll grow up to be a conspiracy theorist. The
government will be out to get me. I'll erase my identity
and move to a South American fishing village but they'll
track me down and drag me back and my parents will
put me in a group home.

I hate technology.

It's a good thing I'm writing everything on good old-
fashioned paper. Someone is going to find this after I'm
gone. When you get to this part and I've disappeared,
go back and watch the video of when I fell. The one
with <u>theraven</u> for a password. Listen to those distant
sounds of metal on metal. I did. I listened to the sounds
over and over again, and now I'll never forget them
even if I try.

Go on. Go back and listen.

Friday, September 17, 10:15 p.m.

I'm feeling less gloomy and more edgy in the last half hour.
Surfing online always has that effect on me. It tends to
fry my nerves. I found an image with all the Morse code
letters and I read all about how the taps and the gaps
in sound are supposed to work.

I figured out that what I heard on the dredge was like
Morse code, but not entirely the same. The longer sound

— the one made by the dash — that one doesn't match up. That's been replaced instead by a different tone. There are two tones on the dredge that represent the dots and the dashes. I imagine the dots being a hammer hitting iron, and the dashes being a wrench hitting the same spot. The two sounds are different in tone instead of length, so it still works.

This is the message that played on the dredge the night I fell:

.- .-. . | -.-- --- ..- | - .... . | .- .-.. -.-. .... . -- .. ... - |

The dots are the hammer, and the bars are the wrench. The message asks a question.

<u>Are you the alchemist?</u>

Eerie, right? I'll admit — I'm freaking out. Because when I was measuring it all out, I didn't think it would add up to anything. I thought it would be nonsense.

But no.

It's a question.

Whatever asked the question was expecting an answer it didn't get. Sarah won't know the answer tonight any better than she did the night of the accident. Maybe the ghost of Old Joe Bush has a message for someone —

the <u>alchemist</u>. It would be useful if I knew what an alchemist was.

And there's the piece of paper I found.

<u>The Alchemist Diagram of 79 for Paul McCray</u>

Paul McCray. That's my dad. So there's no doubt any more. My dad is somehow entangled in this mess, and so is the Crossbones. Was my dad making the sounds? If so, maybe the ghost of Old Joe Bush is trying to make contact, trying to find something or someone.

<u>Are you the alchemist?</u>

What about Daryl Bonner? He looks like Old Joe Bush. He could be the alchemist.

What would happen if I knew the answer and I gave it to Old Joe Bush on the dredge? What would he tell me? What would he do to me?

Whatever it was that made the sounds that night saw Sarah and me as intruders in its secret domain. We didn't understand the question, so we didn't reply. And because of that, it got angry and came for me.

I need to make sure Sarah doesn't go back there again.

She <u>can't</u> go back.

Not ever.

Friday, September 17, 10:41 p.m.

My parents have turned in and Henry is in the guest
room downstairs. It's been a long day of fishing, cards
and comfort food. They'll all be tired. I can't just sit
here. Sarah could already be at the dredge or about
to leave. I have to get out of here. The walk to her
house isn't that far, half a kilometre. I could do it with
my crutches. Maybe. I could tap on her window like the
raven and she'd be safe because she wouldn't go. She's
not the alchemist. She can't go in there if she's not
the alchemist or she might never come out. I could wake
up tomorrow morning and she'd be gone. No one would
know where she went.

Friday, September 17, 11:46 p.m.

I made it to the bottom of the stairs this time. It was dark, so it was slow going, but I made it without knocking anything over. I bumped the coffee table with my cast and it made a sound, but no one stirred.

I opened the front door to the porch as quietly as I could. The screen door remained closed in front of me, and this I knew was a more complicated matter. It's old and squeaky. Another of those home projects my dad never got around to fixing. So I went about opening the screen door very slowly, until there was a gap big enough for me and my lumbering cast to fit through.

It gets really cold at the base of the mountain at night in the autumn — we're at 1,500 metres. I was thinking about how cold it must be — was it 2 or 3 degrees outside? Something like that. Twenty during the day and bitter cold at night — that's autumn in Skeleton Creek.

When I passed through the gap my cast touched the floorboards and they creaked. That's when I heard the voice.

"Hey, partner! Must be hot upstairs. Your mom's got the heat blasting in there."

It was Henry with a bottle in one hand, lying on the old couch, covered in an even older blanket.

"There's no air like this in New York. Not even one breathful."

"I never thought of it that way."

"Well, it's true. When I retire, I'm going to permanently plant my butt on this couch."

"Better talk to my mom. She might sell it."

"She wouldn't. Would she?"

We small-talked a little bit more and then I said I was going back to bed.

"Let me help you up those stairs."

"It's OK — really — I want to do it alone. If you hear a crash, come running. Otherwise, I'll be fine."

"Suit yourself."

I went back inside, past the living room and the dining room and into the kitchen at the back of the house. We have a yellow phone in there that hangs on the wall, and I dialled Sarah's number. I know — stupid — but I was out of options. It was a terrible risk, but I truly felt she was in trouble. If keeping her safe meant giving her up, then I was ready to pay that price.

It rang four times and I almost hung up. Sarah's mom answered. She sounded like I woke her.

"Hello?"

Already it felt like a mistake. But I had to keep going.

"Hi, Mrs Fincher. It's me, Ryan."

"Are you OK? What's wrong?"

"I woke up worried about Sarah. I don't know why. Could you do me a favour and make sure she's OK?"

"Hang on."

There was a long pause in which I thought I would crawl out of my own skin. My parents could come down any second. Sarah could be gone. Henry could walk in...

After about ten years, Sarah's mom came back on the line.

"She's asleep."

"Oh, that's great. OK, I'm fine now — sorry to bother you. Really sorry."

"Ryan, you can't be calling here. You know that."

"Please don't tell my parents — I was just worried — I haven't talked to her in a while."

"How are you holding up?"

"Great! I'm just great, Mrs Fincher. The leg feels much better. Thanks for asking."

"Goodnight, Ryan"

"Night."

I don't think she's going to tell them. Or maybe that's just my hope talking.

I went back to my room as quietly as I could, which took a long time. When I got back into bed, I felt a wave of relief.

Now, reading this over, I'm not sure. I think I did the right thing.

All the other troubles in my life don't matter as long as I know Sarah is safe.

The truth about Skeleton Creek is not worth dying for.

Saturday, September 18, 7:21 a.m.

I don't remember falling asleep. I woke to find this journal sitting at the foot of my bed with the pen tucked inside. Did I do that? I don't think I did. Someone came in here and read it.

There's no other explanation.

I know this because I don't put the pen in like that and because I would never set it on the edge of my bed. It was Dad or Mom. Either way, I'm doomed. It's so much harder to be careful when I'm too tired to keep my eyes open.

Saturday, September 18, 7:35 a.m.

I just checked my email, and Sarah's sent me another video.

Saturday, September 18, 7:38 a.m.

She's driving me crazy! Someone needs to get her under control. I can't believe she actually went to the dredge — and that she's planning on going back.

Doesn't she understand why I called last night?

Doesn't she realize she could get hurt? Or worse?

And I can't believe she's going to make me wait to see what she found out yesterday. That's such a Sarah thing to do — make me feel even more stuck than I felt before. It makes me furious when she holds out on me. She knows that. What I want to do is get my crutches and walk to her house. I'd tell her face-to-face to stop feeding me information with a spoon. What am I, a two-year-old? And while I was at it, I'd tell her to stop being so reckless. It's the same thing all over again, only this time it will be her that gets hurt.

(Is it me, or am I starting to sound a lot like my dad?)

Saturday, September 18, 7:53 a.m.

Sometimes I feel like Sarah is a lit match and I'm a stick of dynamite. Whatever it is that's drawing us together will eventually lead to an explosion.

No, wait — that's not it — it's different. It's more like Sarah and I are polar opposites being pulled towards the same dangerous middle. Why can't we be drawn together by something safe — like raising a cow for the state fair?

Why does everything have to be so dangerous?

Saturday, September 18, 7:53 a.m.

Because a cow is a dull animal and raising one would be a dull undertaking.

Dangerous is more exciting.

Saturday, September 18, 8:35 a.m.

The truth is I'm just mad because I can't stand it that she's having all the adventure and I'm stuck at home with this stupid cast and my meddling parents. She's my best friend and it's hard to be apart and to worry about her. And plus I miss her and I guess I'm lonely.

I'm going online to figure out what an alchemist is.

Saturday, September 18, 8:55 a.m.

I've got a lot of studying to do. Alchemy is ... deep and wide. Precious metals like gold and silver play an important part. Very interesting.

Today I have to drive all the way into the city with my mom to see the doctor. He's on call on Saturday mornings, so it worked out to have Mom drive me when she didn't have to work. We're leaving in half an hour, so I've only had time to print out a chart I found. I'm sticking it in here. I need to send an email to Sarah, too, so she can see this.

He's going to let me get out more — the doctor, I mean. I'm sure of it. Then I'll feel better. Then I can do more. I could be useful. I could look around town for the alchemist or the secret society. I could even go to the dredge if I wanted to.

I've felt this way before. I know what's going on here.

Sarah's dragging me back in again.

Saturday, September 18, 9:15 a.m.

This is what I just wrote to her.

Sarah,

I'm out all day visiting the doctor but I'll be back by six and I'll go straight to my room so I can see what you've found. I wish you'd just told me. When I find things, I tell you right away – why can't you do the same? I understand you want to show me, not tell me, when you discover things, but it's frustrating from over here!

I can get around better. I'm getting used to walking. I'm slow, and stairs are a problem, but I can definitely get out of the house. If you go to the dredge again, I want in. I'm not letting you go out there all by yourself any more. We have to stick together, even if it feels like the whole world is trying to keep us apart.

Someone was sending us a message that night, but we didn't understand it. Do you remember the clanging sounds? Henry told me the workers used to bang on metal to tell each other things because the machinery was so loud. Those sounds that night – they were a question.

Are you the alchemist?

I found the attached file this morning at an alchemy site. I'm not sure what to make of it.

Do you see it? Do you see the birdie?

Let's stay together on this, OK? No more running around at night alone in the woods.

Ryan

And then I showed her the symbols.

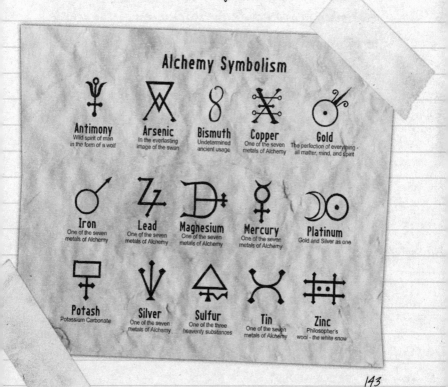

Alchemy Symbolism

Antimony
Wild spirit of man in the form of a wolf

Arsenic
In the everlasting image of the swan

Bismuth
Undetermined ancient usage

Copper
One of the seven metals of Alchemy

Gold
The perfection of everything - all matter, mind, and spirit

Iron
One of the seven metals of Alchemy

Lead
One of the seven metals of Alchemy

Magnesium
One of the seven metals of Alchemy

Mercury
One of the seven metals of Alchemy

Platinum
Gold and Silver as one

Potash
Potassium Carbonate

Silver
One of the seven metals of Alchemy

Sulfur
One of the three heavenly substances

Tin
One of the seven metals of Alchemy

Zinc
Philosopher's wool - the white snow

143

Saturday, September 18, 10:50 a.m.

We have a minivan, which my dad hates and will not drive. I personally like minivans. If you ask me, they get a bad rap. I like that both rows of seats come out and, with the doors shut, a whole sofa fits in there. I can see where that would be handy. And when we go on a long drive, there's room to roam. I don't have to sit in one place all the time. I'm restless, so I appreciate the options.

Having a really long cast on my leg has given me a whole new reason to appreciate the spaciousness of this vehicle. Henry and my dad took the middle seats out and I'm sitting all the way in the back. Plenty of room to rest my leg, and I can write in peace back here. The suspension on this van is really pretty good. A writer can tell.

Saturday, September 18, 1:15 p.m.

OK, I'm alone in the examining room, or whatever they call it.

Since I didn't want to risk anyone seeing the journal, I'm writing this in a regular notebook. I'll paste these pages (and the page from the van) into the journal later.

This was definitely a good idea. Because when I took the notebook out to write about the minivan — not exactly the most controversial of subjects — Mom kept looking in the rear-view mirror. I could tell she wanted to know what I was writing. Maybe she was extra curious because she was the one who sneaked in and looked at my journal before. Maybe she was thinking she'd have to take a look at this new one soon.

It's the pits not being able to trust your own parents.

Finally, while I was writing about the van's suspension, she came right out and asked, "What're you writing there, Ryan?"

"Just stories," I said. "Maybe I'll show them to you one day."

"So you keep telling me."

I pretended to joke with her. "Then you haven't read them?" I said lightly.

Her tone was just as jokey. "Nope. Too busy feeding Henry and sorting mail."

"So I can trust you?"

Then she got all serious.

"It's like faith," she said. "You just have to believe. I can't prove it to you."

This was, I think, a good answer.

"Do you think Dad has read my stories?" I ventured.

She met my eye briefly in the rear-view mirror, then looked back to the road. "If he has, he's the biggest hypocrite in three counties. You know how he respects privacy. Worth its weight in gold, right?"

"Right."

We drove a little bit more in silence. I wondered what she was thinking, because the next thing she asked was, "Have you emailed Sarah?"

I lied and told her I hadn't.

"Trust goes both ways, you know," she said.

I told her I knew.

Being friends with Sarah makes me a liar. There's no way around it.

Why does everything have to be so complicated?

Saturday, September 18, 5:20 p.m.

Driving home now.

Mom is watching. But I'm too far back for her to be able to read anything.

Everything went fine at the hospital. The doctor cut the hard cast off my leg and replaced it with one that straps on even tighter than plaster. He made me promise to keep it on unless I'm in the shower (and even there I have to sit down on a chair). I asked the doctor if I could keep the cast and he said I could. I'm very excited to get home and surprise Henry with it.

The doctor wants me to start walking around more, which is both good and bad since I'll probably be going to the dredge tonight. Good because I'll have a little more mobility with the lighter leg brace, bad because I'm more likely to reinjure myself if I have a reason to run away.

It's been a quiet drive home and I've been thinking about everything. So much has piled up in the past couple of days, I haven't taken the time to try and piece it all together. I'm afraid of going back, especially at night. I don't want to see Old Joe Bush come out of the black pond. What if he grabs me this time? Ever since I told

Sarah I'd go with her, I've been thinking that he'll get me and drag me down into the water with him. What a nightmare.

I feel certain everything is connected, like Sarah said. The dredge, my dad, the Crossbones, the alchemist, the ghost of Old Joe Bush, even Ranger Bonner. I'm starting to work on a theory I'll tell Sarah tonight.

The worst thing I have to face is that the dredge really is haunted, and that I probably have to go back there. I wonder if I'll drag my leg, and Old Joe Bush will think I'm making fun of him. He won't like that.

Saturday, September 18, 7:10 p.m.

There are too many people around. I can't risk checking the computer. I barely made it off the porch!

OK — I'll admit it.

I'm hiding in the bathroom, so I can at least have time to write a few things down.

I am DYING to get to my room and hear from Sarah. I can only hope my mom and dad don't go up there, check my email, and see that Sarah has sent me a video to watch. That would be a catastrophe.

But they're pretty busy right now, so I think I'm OK.

I hope I'm OK.

Henry and Dad caught two monster steelhead today and decided to have a fish feed on the front porch. I hate fish feeds. About a million neighbours have come over with potato salad, coleslaw, baked beans, and potato chips. I've been sitting on the gold couch for over an hour suffering question after question about my accident. Nobody wants to come right out and ask what I was doing at the dredge, but I can tell they want to know. I can tell they have theories.

Nobody mentions Sarah's name. All these neighbours who've seen us grow up together.

Not a single one.

I know I can't stay in here for ever, but it's the only place people will leave me alone. It's cooling down outside, but a fish feed is a big deal in a town as dull as Skeleton Creek. No one's likely to leave until their teeth start chattering.

There's an oppressive feeling of secrecy in the air, and it's intensified by the size of the crowd.

When I was five, Dad took me fishing on the creek. He hooked a nice trout and handed me the rod. We dragged it in together, his big hand over mine on the reel. Then he took the fish off the hook and bashed its head against a rock until it was dead. I cried all the way home.

I always throw all my fish back. After I catch them, I mean — I throw them back.

I'd rather hold a fish underwater after I catch it and let it pump its gills in my hand until it's ready to swim off. I talk to the fish I catch. Be careful now. I'm a nice fisherman, but the next guy might take you home and cook you. Tell your buddies.

It makes me sad the way we kill things without any reason. Why beat the life out of a wild trout when there's perfectly good canned tuna down at the store?

Henry is having a poker party tonight. He was thrilled to have my old cast at his disposal and thanked me endlessly. Cards will probably go until about midnight, which means it won't be safe for me to leave the house for a long time.

I need to tell Sarah.

Gladys the librarian showed up at the fish feed with a bag of carrots. She came over a half hour ago and held one out to me.

"Eat one of these. It'll help you see trouble coming," she said.

All I could sputter out was, "Yes, ma'am."

I got the chills when she turned to go. I was thinking in terms of the Alchemist Diagram of 79.

<u>The floor and 7th, four past the nine on door number two = library attic, enter through the alley door marked 213.</u>

I feel like she's involved. But how?

Our park ranger, Daryl Bonner, also showed up. It was

strange to see him, because I had to pretend I didn't know what he looked like. I actually went out of my way to ask my dad who he was. Luckily, he wasn't wearing a park ranger outfit or anything, so I didn't sound too out of it. He brought a frozen veggie burger with him, and my dad dropped it on the grill like a hockey puck. The two of them talked quietly until Henry came over and gave Bonner a hard time.

"Those are made of dog food," Henry said. "Did you know that?"

"I hadn't heard."

All three of them swigged their drinks and stared at the hockey puck on the grill.

"We just had our fourth player drop out. Care to play cards tonight?"

"I'd be delighted."

"Bring one of those frozen Frisbees. I have an idea I could use one."

Being new in town, Daryl has no idea that Henry might be taping the frozen veggie burger to his forehead before the night is over. I feel a little sorry for him.

And I also feel really strange that we're under the same roof.

I think I'm going to tell my mom I'm tired. Maybe she'll let me go upstairs and lie down.

There's enough noise that it'll make sense for my door to be closed.

I just hope they won't realize it's also locked.

Saturday, September 18, 7:30 p.m.

My clothes smell like fried fish, which makes me mad at Henry and Dad for going on a killing spree on the river today. You'd think grown men would know better.

It doesn't seem like anyone's been in here. I mean, Dad's been with Henry and I've been with Mom. I should be safe. Plus, they assume there's no activity because I haven't been here. But Sarah's sent me a new password. Finally I'll get to see what she hinted at this morning.

Ryan,

Nice detective work on the alchemist chart. Did you know 79 is the chemical element number for gold? I looked it up. I guess it should stand to reason that everything secret in this town would revolve around gold. Do you think there's a hidden stash of it somewhere?

Sorry I've been mysterious about showing you this, but you're right – it had to be shown, not told.

More talk in the video, especially about visiting the dredge. Password: lucywestenra

Sarah

I've heard that name — Lucy Westenra — but I can't place it. Who is that? Peter Quint, I knew — but Lucy ... I know I've heard that name before. I'll have to look it up later.

Now, I have a video to watch.

SARAHFINCHER.COM
PASSWORD:
LUCYWESTENRA

Saturday, September 18, 7:55 p.m.

This is too much.

Sarah thinks Joe Bush was killed by the alchemist.

But we don't know who the alchemist is, or even if there's only one of them.

And she thinks Joe Bush's ghost is guarding something. Well, not exactly guarding. He's haunting the place where the alchemist keeps his secrets. Waiting to take revenge.

But what about the dredge? What about that secret handle she seems to have found, which appears to have vanished between then and now, in a place that was supposedly untouched?

What about what I saw?

She can't go back there.

It's too dangerous.

Especially if she's alone.

I can't believe I'm even thinking of going back.

In my condition.

But there won't be any way to stop her, short of calling in our parents.

And I can't do that.

That would be the end of everything.

I have to get there myself.

It's already dark. Pretty soon someone will be wearing my cast at the poker table, holding their cards with oven mitts. I can go down there and watch for an hour and see if I can guess how late they'll go. Some of the players are pretty old, so hopefully things will break up by midnight. Which will give me over an hour.

OK — I just emailed Sarah. This is what I said.

Sarah,

I'm going with you and that's final. Pick me up in the alley behind the house at 1:45 a.m. I'll be the one with the brace on his leg.

Can't wait to see you.

Ryan

I hope I can escape the house without getting caught.

Saturday, September 18, 10:00 p.m.

I just went downstairs without telling anyone so I could see how fast I'd get to the bottom without making any noise or falling on my face. No one saw me, so I did it twice. The second time was slower and more painful than the first, but that was mostly because I'd just come back up and I was winded. The brace is still big and heavy but I can move a little better. I think I can do this. If I take one of the crutches with me I'll be fine.

When I arrived on the porch, the poker game was in full swing. The burn barrel had been moved up next to the card table, where it blazed with warmth and orange light. Ranger Bonner was wearing a football helmet, and when he nodded in my direction it wobbled up and down over his brow. I felt like everyone was taking turns staring at me, like they were trying to have a good time but my being there made them suspicious. Ranger Bonner and my dad especially. They kept glancing at each other, then at me. It was very unnerving.

I felt like I was ruining Henry's card game, so I lied and said I was turning in for the night. No one tried to stop me.

I give it another hour — two at the most — and my mom will tell everyone to clear out.

No word yet from Sarah. Where is she?

Sunday, September 18, 11:00 p.m.

The card game broke up early and I'm getting a bad case of the shakes. It's dark outside. My window is a sheet of black in which I keep imagining Old Joe Bush's face peering in, watching me, water dripping off his nose. Or is it blood? I can't tell. It's too dark out there.

That's one thing about a very small town: it's extremely dark at night. There are only three street lights and none of them are near my front door. The moon is also absent tonight, so I'm sure the woods will be especially dark.

That is, if I make it to the woods. Getting out of the house is going to be a trick. Our house was built about a million years ago and it makes old house sounds, the kind that wake parents up. There are seven squeaky steps on the staircase alone.

My hands are so clammy I keep having to stop writing and wipe them on my sheet.

I'm not sure I can do this.

Sunday, September 19, 12:10 a.m.

Finally, an email.

Ryan,

Come and see – password: miltonarbogast

Sarah

SARAHFINCHER.COM
PASSWORD:
MILTONARBOGAST

Sunday, September 19, 12:22 a.m.

It appears that I'll be sneaking out of the house tonight to see the one person my parents have forbidden me to associate with. The two of us will wander off into the woods at 1:00 in the morning and cut through a chain so we can break into a condemned structure before they burn it down. And, meanwhile, her camera will be feeding the footage back to her website so that if we don't come back, the authorities can — what was her phrase? — oh, yeah — <u>find our bodies</u>.

Has Sarah lost it?

What am I doing?

If I get caught, my parents won't just move me to a new town, they'll ground me for a hundred years and feed me boiled beans for breakfast, lunch and dinner for the rest of my life.

Even still, I almost wish I'd get caught. The alternative is definitely worse.

The dredge at night. I'm not even there yet and I can already feel the haunted presence of a ghost dragging its leg in my direction, asking me questions I can't answer. And this time, when the ghost of Old Joe Bush comes for me, I won't be able to run away.

Sunday, September 19, 12:30 a.m.

Ryan,

We're on – meet me where I said at one, then we'll go straight to the dredge. Check the webcam from your computer (I'll send you the password in a separate email) and email me back. You should see me waving.

Delete!! — Sarah

Sunday, September 19, 12:33 a.m.

I checked the site and saw her waving and now I have to go. I'm confused by this turn of events.

My hands are shaking and I can hardly hold my pen. I know why I'm shaking so badly. It's the same reason why I have to go to the dredge tonight. I think Old Joe Bush has sneaked into my brain, because there's a nightmare I keep having. Every night I have the nightmare, only I don't tell anyone — I don't even write it down — because it's a really bad one. It's the kind that if someone reads it, they think you're crazy.

Sarah is in the nightmare. We're together on the dredge, going up the decaying stairs. When we reach the top she turns to me and leans in like she's going to kiss me. I'm so surprised by this I lean back and lose my balance and I grab for her arm. The rotted railing breaks free behind me and I can't let her go, even though I try. It's like electricity is holding us together. We're two magnets falling. We roll through the air and she lands beneath me. There is the sound of smashing bones and then I wake up.

Sunday, September 19, 12:39 a.m.

I just had to stop and think for a second.

I remember struggling over the beginning of this story, rewriting it a dozen times.

There was a moment not long ago when I thought: This is it. I'm dead.

I remember how that opening set just the right tone. The reader would know that something bad had happened, but they wouldn't know what it was. Things came easy after that, but were confusing, too. The Sarah nightmare bothered me.

Now I feel as if I'm driving around at night in the middle of nowhere. I've lost my sense of direction. Did I have all the videos before? Have I been retracing my steps and she's already gone? Maybe tonight is the last chapter of a story I've already lived through.

I'm going to assume for the moment that the nightmare of Sarah crushed beneath me is just that — a nightmare — and that all of what I've been writing is real. I'm going to make this guess because if what I've been writing is not the truth, then my mind is trying to hide something from me. If I've been making all this up and something happened to Sarah and it's my fault, then I won't be able to live with myself.

I'm going to stand up and put all my weight on my one good leg and start down the darkened hall towards the stairs. When I look over my shoulder, Old Joe Bush will be outside, staring through my bedroom window with the raven on his shoulder. He'll be watching me leave so that he can go to the dredge ahead of me and wait for my arrival. He's faster on one good leg than I am.

When I reach the opening to the staircase, my heart will be pounding and I'll look down and see that there is no light. It will be a long fall if I miss a step. My hand will be sweaty and it will slide when I hold the banister. I feel like I know this already, like I've done it all before.

Words and sounds will tumble in my troubled mind.

The Crossbones. Are you the alchemist? Daryl Bonner. Gladys with her shotgun. Old Joe Bush. Is that my dad's name on the paper? A kiss. The sound of smashing bones.

And hanging over it all will be the one word — gold. It's all about the gold, I know it is. Someone killed Joe Bush for the gold and now Joe wants revenge. He won't rest until he gets what he wants.

It will be a slow journey through a quiet house and I

have no choice but to leave. I have twenty minutes and it will take every bit to sneak out of here. I want to take this journal with me but I can't. It will mean I've left the story behind for sure and returned to the real world. I'm leaving it folded into my sheets so they'll find it in the morning if I'm not here.

Please — if you find this — go to sarahfincher.com. Use the password <u>tanginabarrons</u>.

There you'll see what happens next to me and Sarah.

I've got to go now.

SARAHFINCHER.COM

PASSWORD

TANGINABARRONS

BOOK TWO

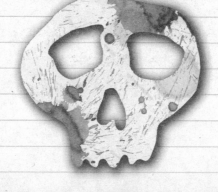

GHOST
IN THE
MACHINE

SARAHFINCHER.COM
PASSWORD:
LEONARDSHELBY

Sunday, September 19, AFTER MIDNIGHT

Am I really doing this?

What's taking her so long?

It's cold in here.

I can't go down there again.

Birdie carved in wood under the gears. Why?

Careful now.

You have been warned.

Remove this Cryptix and suffer the consequences.

When curiosity meets deadly explosive force.

That sound again — not the steps — something else.

Sarah's eyes are big. She's terrified.

I couldn't see it.

I only felt it.

Don't make me come looking for you.

Francis Palmer. Jordan Hooke. Wilson Boyle.

Hector Newton. Joseph Bush. Dad.

Gladys. The Apostle. Dr Watts.

Sunday, September 19, 7:20 a.m.

How did I get back in my room?

The last thing I remember really clearly is standing at the top of the stairs in the dredge and looking down. After that, everything is fuzzy around the edges. Something about seeing my own bloodstain on those old floorboards sort of did me in.

So it was shock. That's it — I was in shock. My brain was smart enough to shut down. I was a zombie, more or less.

I sure looked like one on that video.

I can piece this together. Between the video and my notes from the dredge, I'm sure I can do this. Brand-new journal, brand-new memories. I'm glad I started with a blank slate. It's like a new lease of life. This is totally going to work.

I remember walking up the alley and there she was, standing in the headlights with her camera on. I didn't realize how much I missed seeing her until I shuffled up on my crutches like an idiot and gave her the lamest hug ever.

I remember getting in her car and feeling very nervous

as we left the alley, like I was going to throw up. Sarah didn't want Bonner driving around and seeing her car and maybe coming after us in the middle of the night, so we parked a long way from the start of the trail. This made the endless walk through the woods seem even longer. Let me tell you, dragging a wrapped-up leg through the woods is no picnic. It's a long hoof out there — I mean <u>really</u> long. By the time we got there I was thinking we'd made a big mistake.

I'm sure that's why I scribbled <u>Am I really doing this?</u> at the top of the first page of this new journal. (For obvious reasons, I didn't want to take the old one with me and risk it being lost or, I don't know, captured.) And those next words — <u>What's taking her so long?</u> — I remember those words, too. We'd finally arrived at the dredge, and Sarah left me alone with the camera. I panned it over each of the windows in the dredge while I waited for her to come back and tell me she'd cut the lock on the door. I didn't want to see a ghost in one of those windows, but I couldn't stop looking for one. When Sarah came back, I followed her down the last part of the path.

Before I knew it, we were inside.

<u>It's cold in here.</u>

I remember thinking it was chilly. September in Skeleton Creek is preceded by a long warm summer that lulls you to sleep. Then <u>BANG</u>, the cold nights show up out of nowhere like a screen door in your face.

So it was cold in the dredge, and that's why Sarah was talking with a tiny pattern of starts and stops in her voice. It wasn't because she was afraid. She was cold.

<u>I can't go down there again.</u>

This is where the shock set in, I'm pretty sure. I didn't say I couldn't go down the stairs again, but when we reached the top, I knew I couldn't do it. Stairs were a bad omen in every Alfred Hitchcock movie I'd ever seen, a prelude to something sinister about to happen. And what was much worse, this was the place I'd had the accident and almost died. That was it for me. It was either get out another way or die trying. I remember how it felt to be back there, sort of like someone had cut off the oxygen to my lungs and left me for dead. I floated through the rest and then I woke up in my bed.

I still can't believe everything on that video.

Somehow my zombie form arrived inside the secret room. Seeing that video reminded me of something. I saw the birdie carved in wood. I remember leaning over into the gears instinctively and glancing down into the opening. There's a memory packed in frozen storage somewhere in which I've done this before. I can't crack the ice, but it's there.

What jolted me back to reality? It must have been seeing Sarah turning the dials at the same time I was reading the warning about the whole place exploding. It was like she had a stick of lit dynamite in her hand.

<u>Stop touching it!</u>

I screamed these words, or at least I thought I did. But watching the video, I see that I only screamed in my head. I hate that I can't trust what I saw and what I felt. It's like a repeat of the night I fell, with everything greyed out. I still can't remember the right order or whether certain things happened or not. The scariest thing about watching Sarah's videos is that I don't always know what's coming next.

<u>That sound again.</u>

OK, this I recall perfectly. I've read those three words on the first page of this journal four or five times already, and every time I hear the same sounds. It's like a soundtrack. <u>That sound again, that sound again, that</u>

<u>sound again</u>. I can't describe it, but I heard it at least twice in the video. Once when we were in the alley and once when I saw the birdie. I need to watch that video again because I can't say for sure if the sound is really there or not. It's like I see things — the ghost or the birdie — and I hear the sound. Am I hearing it in my head? Is there some sort of visual cue that's making my brain create the sound? Or is the sound really there?

I scribbled the names. All of them. But here's the strange part: I don't remember when I wrote the names down. It's an awful lot to remember, all those names, but I don't think I wrote them until later. Believe it or not, I think I woke up in the dark in my own bed and did it. I've actually done this before, when I was small. I used to do it all the time. I'd wake up when I was five or six years old and find that I'd drawn the words <u>green egz ham</u> in crayon on the wall in the middle of the night.

"Why did you do that?" my dad would ask in the morning.

"I was asleep. Someone else did it."

"We've told you not to write on your walls," Dad would say, all stern like he was going to punish me.

"I didn't do it," I'd insist.

"Is that so? Then who did?"

"Did you lock the doors last night?"

My dad (and my mom, for that matter) knew then what they know now: I could talk them into their graves if they let me. I could go on and on about whether they locked the windows and checked every room and flushed the toilets and a hundred other things that might or might not have to do with how my walls got covered in purple crayon.

"Stop writing on your walls."

That's all my dad had the energy to say once he could see I was heading down a path that might take twenty minutes and would lead absolutely nowhere.

Most of the time, or so it seems to me, if Dad says anything in my general direction, it's either a warning or a reprimand. I have come to accept this fact, which technically speaking is pretty sad.

At least he never yells at me.

So anyway, this idea of sleepwriting like someone might sleepwalk, I think it might have revisited me last night. Because I'm just about sure I didn't consciously write those names on the front page. Looking at the scrawled names, I'm asking myself, just like my dad used to ask: Why did you do that?

Francis Palmer. Jordan Hooke. Wilson Boyle. Dr Watts. Who are these people? And what about Hector Newton and The Apostle — who are they? I've never heard of a single one of them, so why are their names carved in stone inside a secret room on the dredge?

And while we're at it, why is my dad's name hidden in that room right under Joe Bush's name? And the local librarian?

Sarah's eyes are big. She's terrified.

I couldn't see it.

I only felt it.

I'm glad I didn't see Old Joe Bush for myself when we were trapped in the secret room. I'm glad I was wedged in there, facing the wall so I couldn't turn around. Seeing a ghost on video is bad enough; I don't need to see it in person.

Later in the car — I sort of remember this conversation now — Sarah said it was the scariest thing she'd ever seen, like whatever terrible thing was out there had her trapped and wanted her dead. She said the ghost of Old Joe Bush sniffed the air, which I didn't really get from watching the video, but that's how she felt about it. When he leaned in, she saw his face and almost screamed. She'd wanted to scream, but Old Joe Bush was almost touching the back of my head and she was completely paralysed with fear.

I remember something else now, something horrible. I remember at that moment it felt extra cold, like a giant block of ice was about to touch the back of my neck.

But I didn't turn around. I didn't get to see it until I watched the video a few minutes ago. The more I remember, the more I wish Sarah had never shown it to me.

There's a big gap now, a whole section I just don't remember at all. I don't remember getting out of the secret room or coming to the stairs and insisting once again that I couldn't go down. I don't remember racing through parts of the dredge I'd never seen before or cowering in the corner. I absolutely don't recall getting back up and making myself hobble forward until we came to the way out.

<u>Don't make me come looking for you.</u>

A message smeared on the door. The kind of words that say <u>Don't you dare tell the cops, don't tell your</u>

parents, don't trust anyone in this town, and, most of all, don't ever come back into the dredge again.

That I remember. I remember it more than anything else from last night, for the worst possible reason. I remember it because when I woke up this morning, I got out of bed and shuffled over to my desk. When I turned around, I saw that I'd scrawled those very words on the wall over my bed.

It's very disturbing when you come to the realization that you've been awake without knowing it, doing bizarre things you can't recall.

Then again, maybe I didn't write the message on the wall over my bed.

It could be someone else's writing.

I guess it could be my dad's or Ranger Bonner's.

Or, more likely, the ghost of Old Joe Bush followed me home so he could make sure I understood him the first time.

Sunday, September 19, 8:15 a.m.

I just spent the last twenty minutes standing on my bed with a wet rag, scrubbing words off the wall. Ink is a lot harder to wash off than a purple crayon. It's especially difficult because my leg is still killing me and standing on my bed without falling off is a real trick.

For some reason the word <u>Don't</u> was darker than all the other words, so it reads more like **<u>Don't</u>** <u>make me come looking for you</u>. But it didn't really matter, because twenty minutes of scrubbing did almost nothing to remove the words. What I really need is some sandpaper and a can of paint.

I moved my <u>Dark Side of the Moon</u> poster to cover the message. I haven't even noticed that poster for months and months — I think I only ever listened to Pink Floyd for about a week in the eighth grade to begin with. I have no idea why I still have it hanging in my room.

My mom came in a few minutes later and stood over my bed, staring at the poster I'd moved.

"I used to listen to that music when I was your age," she said. "Did I ever tell you that?"

She'd told me about a thousand times, so I nodded.

"Why did you move it?"

I shrugged and changed subjects, hoping she wouldn't notice I'd pinned it up slightly crooked and try to fix it.

"I think I'll stay in bed a little longer. I didn't sleep so well last night."

Mom was still staring at the poster, like it brought back some memory she hadn't had in a while. Then she looked down at me.

"Your dad wants you out of this room and doing something with your life. Back to school in only a week, remember? You've really got to get used to walking on that leg."

If only she'd known how far out of my room I'd been the night before. I gave her my tired look, which wasn't hard because I was exhausted.

She sighed. "I can hold him off for another half hour with bacon and eggs." Then she went to the door and turned back for one more look at the poster. "You know it's crooked, right?"

I closed my eyes like I was dozing off and nearly fell asleep by accident.

When the door was shut and I was sure she was gone, I pulled my phone out from under my pillow. Sarah had said 8:30 a.m. and it was 8:30 a.m. There was a one-word text message on my screen, which I recognized from one of my favourite books. Does Sarah think I'm losing my grip on reality, just like Jack Torrance did? I wish I could remember everything from last night, but I can't. Maybe I am going crazy and I just don't know it. I suppose if I were losing my marbles, I'd be the last one to know.

I deleted the password, went to my desk, and logged on to Sarah's site.

SARAHFINCHER.COM
PASSWORD:
JACKTORRANCE

Sunday, September 19, 11:00 a.m.

I couldn't go back to sleep after watching Sarah's newest video... and I was hungry besides. The breakfast smell working its way up the stairs and under my door is tough to ignore, especially on Sunday morning when we actually get a weekly paper and Mom doesn't give me a hard time about drinking coffee. Any other morning she's on my case, but Sunday is a free pass for reasons I don't entirely understand.

Have you ever looked across the table, past a plate of scrambled eggs, bacon and toast, and wondered if you could trust your own parents?

I just did.

"Where's Henry?" I said, and then I shoved most of a piece of toast in my mouth and washed it down with coffee.

"Fishing," Dad said. He was staring at the paper, which was on the table next to his plate. He glanced up at me, then back at the editorial page. "You're going to school next week," he went on.

"I know."

"That's not a licence to talk with Sarah Fincher. You know that, right?"

I didn't answer him. Inside I was seething, but there was no point saying anything. I was already talking with Sarah practically every day without either of my parents knowing about it. Getting their permission had found its way to the bottom of my priority list.

Mom piped in. "He knows, Paul. Just read your paper and let the boy eat in peace."

"All right, all right. But we agreed. School next week, no excuses. And no Sarah Fincher."

They still blamed Sarah for my accident. They said she was trouble.

They were totally wrong about the first part.

The second part remained to be seen.

I finished my breakfast and came back to my room. I could tell Dad wanted to insist I go outside, but Mom was pretty mad about how he was badgering me, so he left me alone. I think I've got a few hours of peace and quiet up here, at least until Henry gets back. After that, all bets are off. He'll want to play cards or talk.

What's my dad hiding? His name is on a slab in the dredge that ties him to a whole bunch of other names. He's part of a secret society. He's got the alchemy symbol for gold tattooed on his shoulder and that alchemist diagram in his drawer.

It has to add up to something. But what?

I'll start with the names from the secret room — that's my best clue. I'll work my way down the list and figure out who these people are.

Maybe some of them are still alive.

Like the librarian.

Like my father.

Sunday, September 19, 2:00 p.m.

Other than my mom stopping by an hour ago with lunch, I've had three hours of uninterrupted research time on my laptop. I keep it very quiet in my room — no music or anything like that — so I could hear the ting of a butter knife on the edge of a glass mayonnaise jar as she made my sandwich. This was my signal to erase everything I was working on. I can now do this and re-enable the software my parents think is keeping tabs on me in less than thirty seconds. Unless they're watching with a camera, there's no way they're keeping track of what I'm doing up here.

I almost spilled the beans to my mom when she was in here. It's like I want to trust her, but she's married to my dad and he's tangled up in this secret stuff. She'd tell him. I know she would. And she was just as mad at me after the accident. Maybe madder.

After Mom set the Coke and the sandwich on my desk, she stared out of the window.

"You coming down anytime soon?"

I shrugged and popped the top on the Coke can.

"Is Henry back yet?" I asked.

My mom shook her head. "Your dad went after him. Fishing must be good."

I hesitated a second, then said, "Have you ever been in the old dredge, Mom?"

She looked at me like I was slipping through her fingers and falling down a steep hill. You know the look. The one where your mom thinks you're in trouble but can't help you.

"I haven't been out to the dredge in years. Why do you ask?"

I could see she was nervous, like I was dancing around the edge of something she was afraid to hear. So I totally backed off.

"No reason. It's been out there a long time. I figured you'd been inside."

She looked relieved, which made me glad I hadn't told her I was seeing ghosts, hanging out with Sarah, and wandering around the dredge in the middle of the night getting trapped in secret rooms. My mom wanted a normal son, who was in school and didn't get into strange kinds of trouble all the time. I can't really say that I blame her.

"Eat your sandwich," she said, and then we talked

about something else. (It'll make more sense if I explain it later. But we did talk some more.)

Then she left and I was all alone.

That was the only interruption I had in a very successful three hours online, as detective work goes.

Here's what I did:

First I made a list of all the names that were on the slab in the secret room. I added Daryl Bonner's name to the list because I don't trust him at all. Neither does Sarah. The names became, I guess, my suspect list. Suspects of what crime, I don't know — yet.

But I'm closer to finding some answers now than I was last night.

This was the list I began with, in the order I wanted to investigate them:

Joseph Bush

Francis Palmer

Paul McCray

Gladys Morgan

The Apostle

Dr Watts

Jordan Hooke

Wilson Boyle
Hector Newton
Daryl Bonner

First things first: scratch Joseph Bush from the list.

That guy is already dead.

I went back to my old journal and read my entry from September 13th. I've torn it out and moved it here as evidence:

The greatest discovery — or the worst, depending on how you look at it — that Sarah and I made involved the untimely death of a workman on the dredge. There was only one mention of the incident in the newspaper, and nothing anywhere else. Old Joe Bush is what they called him, so I can only conclude that he was not a young man. Old Joe Bush had let his trouser leg get caught in the gears, and the machinery of the dredge had pulled him through, crushing his leg bone into gravel. Then the dredge spit him out into the grimy water. His leg was demolished, and under the deafening sound in the dark night, no one heard him scream.

Old Joe Bush never emerged from the black pond below.

Whenever I see or hear that name, my leg starts to ache and I think of all the times I've seen and heard what remains of Old Joe Bush. I've heard him with my own ears, dragging that crushed leg across the old floor of the dredge. I've seen footage of him — am I really saying this? — seen him through the broken window and leaning down into the secret room and moving across a camera that's been dropped. I've felt him push me over a rail, high enough off the ground to kill me.

The important thing right now is that Joseph Bush is off the list. And he's not the only worker who died on the dredge. I searched and searched for Francis Palmer and didn't have any luck at all until I remembered all those minutes and reports from the New York Gold and Silver Company. Those were big files and there were lots of them, plus I had gone in and started highlighting different areas of interest. I couldn't keep those files on my computer, so I'd transferred them to a flash drive and taped it under one of the drawers to my desk.

And you know what? It's a good thing I did that. Because when I went looking for those files online a couple of hours ago, a big chunk of them were gone. Someone, somewhere, was able to classify those old files or knew someone was looking at them. Maybe they tracked my IP address to Skeleton Creek and didn't like someone snooping around. It's not a good sign that things from the past are being hidden away. People only hide reports if they think someone will find something bad in them.

Which is exactly what I found.

I pulled up the files from that flash drive and ran a program I have that will sift through multiple documents for key words all at one time. I put in the key words <u>Francis Palmer.</u> I got a return on a document dated within months of the death of Joseph Bush. When I highlighted the entry from a board of directors meeting, I realized

the death of Francis Palmer took place only twenty-seven
days after the death of Joseph Bush.

NYGS PM Mins. -- Paragraph 9, page 25.

The #42 asset holding in Skeleton Creek, Oregon,
was the location of a fatal accident on 8-12-63. The
second fatality in less than a month has led to an
internal safety and structural investigation of
assets #31-#47. The victim, Francis Palmer, was a
long-term night shift control room operator. He was
found dead in the water below asset #42, an apparent
accidental drowning. Legal department advises adding safety precautions to asset #42 in the form of
railings and window bars. Approved. Cost analysis
for modifications to asset #42 scheduled for 9-15.
Insurance claims pending with Palmer family.

Scratch Francis Palmer off the list.
    Dead.
    He and Joe Bush were both in the Crossbones and
both of them died on the dredge within a month of each
other. I had a brief moment of concern as my dad's face

197

flashed before my eyes. Twenty per cent of the people on the list had already been killed off, and I hadn't even been investigating for an hour.

The next two people on the list were Dad and Gladys Morgan, the librarian. I at least know these two are still alive. For some reason I just couldn't go searching around online for my dad. It was too weird. Who knew what kind of junk I might dig up about Paul McCray? He was involved, he was alive, he was secretive like everyone else in town, he'd lived here his whole life, he had a diagram with symbols and strange statements on it, he had a secret tattoo, and he was living in the same house as me.

So I moved on to Gladys Morgan, expecting to find out she was a dreary old windbag with a long, eventless life full of long, eventless days, weeks and months.

Boy, was I wrong.

The first thing I found? Gladys Morgan hasn't always stayed in Skeleton Creek, contrary to what she tells everyone. She also spent some time in New York City, if you can believe that. How do I know Gladys Morgan was in New York City? Because the *New York Times* is archived online, and Gladys Morgan once made the news. That's right — <u>our</u> Gladys Morgan — in the *New York Times*! And here's the most interesting part: she was in the news right after the accidents on the dredge occurred.

Here's a small part of the article I found:

PROTEST ERUPTS OVER ENVIRONMENTAL ALLEGATIONS

New York Gold and Silver board members arrived on Park Avenue this morning and found more than fifty protesters from all across America. The company, which operates dozens of gold dredges in remote parts of Alaska, Oregon and Montana, has come under fire in recent months for what many are calling a disregard for environmental concerns in small towns across the West.

One of those in attendance, Gladys Morgan, came all the way from rural Oregon to join in the protest.

"They've got some explaining to do, simple as that," Morgan said. She, like many of those in attendance, lives in a small town where a New York Gold and Silver dredge grinds along the outskirts of town twenty-four hours a day, seven days a week. "They haven't kept up their end of the bargain. I'm here to tell them they're gonna, whether they like it or not."

Jim Pearson, a lumber mill worker from Billings, Montana, who drove the entire 3,000-mile journey with his dog, Skipper, had similar complaints.

What was she doing there? I get that she was angry, but going all the way to New York to complain with a bunch of other small-town folks? I think there was more to it than that. What if she was there as a member of the Crossbones? Two of them were dead in the span of a month. Or maybe the whole thing was a cover, especially her participation in this rally, and she worked for New York Gold and Silver all along. She could have killed them both. It's possible. She sure has the temper for it.

In detective terms, I think the evidence clearly points to Gladys Morgan as a person of interest.

The next name on my list, The Apostle, led nowhere. I couldn't find anything online that made any sense or connected anyone with that title to Skeleton Creek or the dredge. The only thing I can think of now is to check with one of the old churches in town. Maybe they know something. With a name like The Apostle, a house of worship seems like the most obvious place to look.

Dr Watts — now that one's interesting. He was surprisingly easy to find in the Skeleton Creek historical archives. I was right in the middle of working on this lead when I heard my mom making the sandwich downstairs. That's why, when I went down there, I steered the conversation to Dr Watts, because I figured she would have heard of him. When I mentioned his name, she cringed.

"That old geezer?" she said. "He had the worst bedside manner of any doctor I've ever met. And he hated kids. I know, because I was one of his patients."

"Is he still alive?" I asked.

"Far as I know. I guess he retired about twenty years ago, before you were born. He'd be about eighty by now. He's reclusive. But he lives right off Main Street."

"You mean he doesn't get out much?"

"I mean he _never_ gets out. At least I haven't seen him. Mary over at the store delivers his groceries and cleans up after him. She says he's obsessed with alchemy. You know what that is?"

I shook my head, not wanting her to know how much or how little I knew. The fact that Dr Watts was into alchemy was a big deal.

"Well, it's sure not good medicine. Something about mixing metals or chemicals. I think it's making him soft in the head, whatever it is."

Very interesting. Dr Watts is alive, so that makes three. And, just as important, he's messing around with alchemy, which has to be connected to the alchemy chart I found in my dad's dresser.

And speaking of threes — the last three names on the list inside the dredge were connected. Here's how I figured it out:

First I searched each of the names separately: Jordan Hooke, Wilson Boyle, Hector Newton. The searches for those names didn't lead anywhere interesting. Then I put all three names in at one time and searched them together. To my surprise, things started adding up. It was only the last names that mattered, and it quickly became clear that the first names were bogus, placed there to throw an outside observer off the track. Jordan, Wilson, and Hector were there for show, but Hooke, Boyle, and Newton? Those were incredibly interesting last names when taken together.

Sir Isaac Newton — obviously I'd heard of him. Gravity and all. But the other two — both with the first name Robert — were even more interesting. Robert Hooke and Robert Boyle were contemporaries of Newton's and often worked right alongside him (if not in his enormous shadow). All three scientists were fiercely competitive and laid claim to similar finds.

Here's where the dots start to connect: Boyle in particular was a great enthusiast of alchemy. It was a secret fascination. As I read more about it, I began to understand that alchemy is, at least in part, the science of trying to turn one kind of metal into another. Boyle — I almost fell out of my chair when I read this — was totally obsessed with the properties of one thing in particular: gold.

Alchemy, gold, the dredge, the Crossbones, Dr Watts — these things are all connected somehow. And that chart in my dad's dresser drawer, The Alchemist Diagram of 79 for Paul McCray.

Henry and my dad are going to be home soon. I should go downstairs and sit on the porch so they don't wonder what I'm doing up here. No sense getting them suspicious when I don't have to.

This is what I have so far:

Joseph Bush — dead

Francis Palmer — dead

Paul McCray — my dad, alchemy chart

Gladys Morgan — New York visit

The Apostle — send Sarah to check the churches

Dr Watts — alive, alchemy, reclusive

~~Jordan Hooke~~ — fabricated
~~Wilson Boyle~~ — fabricated
~~Hector Newton~~ — fabricated
Daryl Bonner — shows up mysteriously, can't be trusted

A few hours' work and I've cut the list in half.
Not bad.

Sunday, September 19, 10:00 p.m.

It's clear my parents are serious about keeping me out of my room. And they've enlisted Henry to help them.

Is it really ten?

I'm tired.

As soon as I got out on the porch, Henry and my dad came back home. They'd caught a slew of fish (September is always good up here on the creek) and they didn't let up for almost an hour talking about this fly pattern and that rising fish and the one that got away. This is a little bit like watching a golf tournament on television, more background noise than anything that requires serious concentration.

About half an hour into this endless stream of fish talk, my mom informed me that Randy and Dennis were coming over for HBs with their parents. This was not good news. Randy and Dennis are brothers who live in town. My mom keeps trying to set us up, sort of like a playdate for teenagers.

These guys are about as interesting as dirt. We have exactly zero things in common, plus they're loud and they like to beat each other up. I'm not even saying they're bad people, exactly — just that I can't think of a single reason why I would want to spend my Sunday evening listening to them talk about video games, dirt bikes and farts.

But they showed up anyway because I couldn't bring myself to tell Mom to cancel and, truthfully, it was almost worth it for the HB.

An HB, in case I die and this journal is found in a ditch somewhere a hundred years from now, is a Henry Bomb. This is a burger that is huge beyond all reason. Part of the fun of having an HB is to see how much of it you can eat. No one, to my knowledge, has ever finished a Henry Bomb. My mom and Randy and Dennis's mom split <u>half</u> of one HB, if that tells you anything. And my mom is no slouch. She can put away a Whopper no problem. But this thing? Half an HB is like a whole meat loaf.

Our grill is pretty good size, but Henry only cooks one Henry Bomb at a time because they're extraordinarily "made to order". Tomatoes, lettuce, onions, special sauce (it's a secret, it's orange, and it's awesome), every kind of pepper, about a dozen ziplock bags filled with seasoning salt of varying degrees of heat (<u>total wimp</u> all the way up to <u>blow your head off</u>). Don't even get me started on the

HB buns, which Henry makes himself from frozen bread dough (think Frisbee and you're in the ballpark).

I tried and failed to eat an entire HB.

It took a long time.

Just checked my phone and Sarah texted me:

9 EMV at 630am. MU EL

Delete.

Nine means her parents are watching. They must be paying closer attention than usual. Emailing Video at 6:30 a.m., she misses me, ends with Evil Laugh.

Actually, I'm sort of glad she's not sending me a video until tomorrow morning. Half the time I get these things at night and then I can't sleep.

I'm taking five minutes to write her an update on alchemy and The Apostle and everything else I figured out, and then it's lights out.

Monday, September 20, 6:30 a.m.

Monday morning. Exactly one week from now I'll be getting ready for school. Maybe classes and homework will make my life feel normal again.

The second I woke up, I sat up and looked at all the walls in my room. There was no new writing. Either I couldn't find a pen in my sleep last night (this is possible since I made a point of putting every pen I have at the back of a drawer and shutting it tight) or whoever wrote the first message doesn't feel like he needed to tell me twice.

And then there was this other, worse feeling as I woke up and looked at the poster I moved. If I lifted it and looked underneath, would the words even be there?

<u>Don't Make Me Come Looking For You</u>.

This is how messed up my memory is becoming.

Can I even tell the difference between truth and fiction?

I checked my phone — no password. I checked my email — no password. Then I looked out the window and saw a piece of paper was taped to the outside.

This can't be good.

I pulled the window up just far enough to reach my hand under and take the note.

I could hear my parents talking down the hall, getting ready to leave for work. Henry would sleep in late and probably go fishing. Pretty soon I'd have the house to myself.

Here's what the note said:

No more email or text messaging for a couple days! My parents are really cracking down. Bonner stopped by here yesterday — Sunday, can you believe that? He told my parents someone had cut the lock on the dredge and gone back in. He came right out and said he suspected it was me. Unbelievable. He kept giving me the evil eye, like when I was in his office the other day. It's a good thing I grabbed those bolt cutters on the way out or we'd be finished. Don't be surprised if he shows up at your front door.

I got your message about the alchemy —
veeeeery interesting. I wish we could sit down
and talk! It's killing me. I'll do some digging at
the church on the edge of town after school. For
now, I've got some big news of my own — just
go to the site and use <u>castleofotranto</u> as the
password. I have to get back to my house before
it gets light outside.

I can't wait to see you! But don't send any
more emails or texts — at least for today — it's
too risky. Leave me messages at the blue rock
like we used to when we were kids and I'll do the
same.

Sarah

P.S. I heard you had Henry Bombs last night.
<u>Everyone</u> heard. I'm so mad I couldn't be there. I
bet you tried to eat a whole one since we couldn't
split it, didn't you?

That might be the best password yet. Very impressive.

And she's right. I did miss having her there to eat half
my dinner. Being a glutton about it didn't make me any
less lonely. Plus I got a stomach ache.

The blue rock. A hassle, but at least it'll be safer with Daryl Bonner snooping around. Ever since that guy came to town a few weeks ago, there's been nothing but trouble. What's his real reason for transferring here?

I can hear people in the house.

Dad's shaving, Mom is making coffee.

I better show myself. Then I'll come back and check the video.

Monday, September 20, 7:45 a.m.

Parents are gone and Henry is still asleep downstairs.
   Time to check that video.

SARAHFINCHER.COM
PASSWORD:
CASTLEOFOTRANTO

Monday, September 20, 8:15 a.m.

I really hope that all librarians aren't like Gladys Morgan. Because I'd really like, at some point, to walk into a library and not be afraid for my life.

It definitely looked like she was trying to hide that wooden crow. But why bother? I've seen it dozens of times over the years and never thought twice about it. I even remember thinking it was crooked once and thinking someone should nail it up there tighter so it wouldn't fall off if the wind blew down Main Street.

It's funny how you can look at something and ascribe no meaning to it for ever and ever. Then one day you see it in a completely different way. That wooden crow has sat quietly turning for years while no one paid any attention.

<u>Almost</u> no one.

My dad was paying attention. So was Gladys. Old Joe Bush and Francis Palmer <u>used</u> to pay attention, before they died.

I wonder when the crow is going to turn again . . . and when it does, who will do the turning?

Monday, September 20, 10:10 a.m.

Henry wandered up here with a cup of coffee. He didn't exactly startle me when he came in, but Henry doesn't really knock so much as barge. He was standing in the doorway when I realized I had a bunch of names from the secret room written on a piece of paper next to my laptop. Some of the names were scratched out because I'd discovered they were dead.

I set my elbow on the list.

Henry already had his fishing boots on, which my mom hates because they smell like a mouldy loaf of bread. He's not supposed to wear them in the house. It made me wonder if he'd worn them to bed.

He started talking to me the second he entered the room.

"I sleep like the dead up here in the mountains. You?"

I nodded and Henry looked around the room. His eyes locked on the *Dark Side of the Moon* poster.

"How come you moved that?"

"Trying to change things up, I guess."

"I remember one of those songs. Used to get stuck in my head a lot."

And then he sang a verse off-key, which sort of freaked me out. It was the one about the rabbit running and digging holes and never getting to stop. I think Henry was half amazed he could remember the words.

"I can hear that song in my head like it was yesterday," he said. Then he was a little sad — an emotion I'd almost never seen him display.

"Two more days and it's back to the city for old Henry," he went on. "Time to dig another hole, I guess, like the good song says."

"Why don't you just quit and come live here with us?" I asked. "I think my dad would like that."

"For starters, your mother would kill me. Me and my boots and poker and dragging your dad out to the river. A week a year is pushing things as it is."

"My mom loves you," I said. And I meant it.

"I'm easy to love for a couple of weeks. It gets a little harder after that."

He laughed this comment off, but I think deep down he was serious.

I'd never really thought of it that way, but I could see he might have a point. The charm of an old bachelor like Henry probably wears thin after a while. I don't mind him hogging all the time with Dad, but if he were here all the time? I'd mind. I like Henry's loud voice and his energy and the way he can get everyone to play cards. But there's a twitch that sets in after a couple of weeks when it starts to feel like he's almost annoying.

Henry's smarter than he knows, to leave us wanting more and never overstay his welcome.

I decided to ask him a question.

"You ever talk to Gladys, the librarian?"

Henry was leaning against the door jamb. It appeared he was trying to remember the next verse to the song he'd sung.

Finally, he refocused. "I haven't said a word to Gladys Morgan in ten years. Me and her had a run-in. If I see her coming, I head for the other side of the street."

I thought this sounded like there might be a good story, so I prodded him.

"What happened? What did she do?"

"Let's just say she's not as patient as your mom. I stepped into her precious library with my wet boots on, just off the stream. Sloshed right up to her desk and asked if she had anything on barbecuing a pig."

"You're kidding."

"Nope. She looked me up and down like I'd picked up her cat and thrown it in front of a moving truck. That woman can glare better than all the New York ladies that've turned me down for a date. So she glared, then — get this — she got out of her chair, came around the desk, and kicked me."

"She didn't."

"Not only that, but she told me I better take my stupid pig and my wet boots and go outside and never come back. I told her I didn't exactly have the pig with me, it was just something I was thinking about. That didn't go over too well."

The scary thing was, I can totally picture all this happening. "What'd she say when you told her you didn't have the pig?" I asked.

"She said if it was between me and a chicken and she could only save one of us, she'd definitely save the chicken."

Henry laughed his big laugh again, and I laughed, too.

That Gladys Morgan, what a kook.

I was feeling bold, so I kept going.

"You ever see Dr Watts?" I asked.

"He's dead," said Henry.

"No, he's not. Mom said so."

Henry scratched his stubbly face.

"I thought he was dead. I haven't seen him in forever. You sure he's alive?"

"That's what Mom said."

Henry seemed a little perplexed.

"Well, if she says so."

Henry looked at the Pink Floyd poster again, and I was sure he'd see it was crooked and want to move it.

"You see that story in the paper about the dredge?" he said.

Henry had been sensitive to my accident there and didn't mention it much.

"Yeah," I said. "They're burning it down."

"It's a shame I'm leaving so soon. Hate to miss the biggest bonfire in three counties. But you know how some people feel about me around here. Probably best if I'm gone when the old relic finally gets what's coming to it."

I know I've mentioned this before, but Henry used to work for New York Gold and Silver. He'd come out when the dredge was running, way back in the day, to keep an eye on #42. He hated what the dredge did to the land, but he was young and ambitious back then. He told me as much. He wanted a big career at a big company in a big city, just like a lot of people.

Skeleton Creek stayed in his bones long after New York Gold and Silver went bankrupt. Some say Henry keeps spending all his vacation time here because he feels bad about working for a company that almost destroyed the town. I think he comes here because his best friend is here — my dad — and because he loves the mountains.

I felt a little sorry for Henry when he peeled himself from my room and went downstairs. I heard the screen door flap against the wall and knew he'd gone to the creek.

So now I'm alone in the house again, and I can't help thinking about what it feels like to live in Skeleton Creek. I've been trying to put my finger on it for a long time. No one new ever moves here. It's the same old people keeping mostly to themselves. There's a kind of Gothic loneliness about everything.

You know what it feels like?

It feels like the dredge dug the heart out of my town and chucked it into the woods. All that's left are the ghosts walking around.

Monday, September 20, 4:10 p.m.

Well, my parents can't complain about me sitting in my room all day. Henry came back and talked me into going down to the creek with my fly rod. I haven't been up to fishing since before the accident and I probably had no business standing anywhere near fast-moving water with a shattered leg barely out of a full leg cast.

Henry did most of the casting, catching, hooting and hollering. I mostly sat in the shade and watched him work his way up and down the best stretches of Skeleton Creek, hooking fish after fish. I have to give him credit: He'd learned the water and knew what to throw. I've been fishing nothing but Skeleton Creek all summer for years and I've never caught as many big fish as I saw Henry catch today. The guy is a machine.

Being out near the water today made me value it more than ever. The creek is lined with these great big cottonwood trees that fill the air with what looks like snow every time the wind blows. And there are groves of aspen – thin trees with white bark and gold leaves – huddled close along the banks of some of the best water. Those aspen groves will take your breath away. And there's one other thing, a part of this place that makes it unlike any other. All those big piles of rock and earth the dredge dug up formed an endless line of rolling hills along the banks of the creek. Over the years the surface filled with grass and trees and flowering plants. The creek is like a secret paradise no one has discovered way up here, tucked away in the woods next to a ramshackle town the size of a postage stamp. There are birds everywhere, little creatures scampering and chirping over the hills, and larger animals rustling in hidden places nearby.

All these sights and sounds today made me realize how much I missed visiting the creek. It gave me a view of things I hadn't thought of before. I'd only ever hated the dredge like everyone else. But right here, right under my nose, is this spectacular thing the dredge left behind. It makes me wonder if this is a principle that can be counted on: good things can be created from bad.

I can't stop thinking about how this old town of mine just needs a lucky break to start heading in the right direction again.

Monday, September 20, 7:25 p.m.

Sometimes, after one of Henry's barbecues or a morning at the café eating chicken-fried steak and eggs, my mom decides the McCrays need to eat a healthy dinner. This is a terrible idea and always puts my dad in a bad mood.

"Just eat. It's not going to kill any of you."

These were my mom's words as my dad, Henry and I sat staring at the food she'd placed before us.

"What is it?" Henry was brave enough to ask. He was about half serious and half honestly curious as he stared at the three bowls clustered together in the middle of the table.

"That right there is rice," I said, pointing to the round bowl in the middle.

"It's <u>brown</u> rice," my mom corrected, staring at Henry. "Are you going to tell me you've never seen rice before?"

Henry had seen rice. It was the main dish he was worried about.

"What about that stuff?" he asked.

He pointed to a bowl filled with something that looked like green logs floating in a purple lake.

"You really want to know?" asked my mom. "Because you're eating it whether I tell you or not."

Henry pondered his options, swallowed hard and nodded. "Tell me."

My mom scooped up a big spoonful of brown rice and slapped it on to Henry's plate, then she ladled a glob of purple lake water and green sticks over the top.

"Low-fat yoghurt with whole beets, pulverized in a blender and poured over a can of green beans. Eat up."

Henry looked like he was about to barf.

The last item was a flat pan of green jelly with sad little mandarin oranges trapped all through the middle. My dad put about half the pan of jelly on his plate so there was no room for anything else, and then he sat there, slurping miserably with a spoon.

"Stop that," my mom said. She can't stand it when people slurp their jelly.

The best part was when Mom took a bite of this crazy concoction and chewed and chewed but couldn't swallow without washing it down with a Diet Coke. She tried really hard to keep a straight face, but once Henry took a bite himself, just to be a good sport, his eyes started bulging and Mom came completely unglued.

We all had a pretty good laugh and then she let Henry and my dad go to the kitchen and make pancakes for dinner.

We sat there — me and my mom — eating jelly without slurping.

"You doing OK?" she asked.

"Yeah. It was nice going to the creek today. I haven't done that for a while."

"I'm glad you went outside. The fresh air is good for you."

I nodded and took another bite of green jelly.

"I checked your computer last night," she said. "It looked clean — a little too clean, if you get my drift."

Uh-oh. Maybe my mom knows more about computers than I thought. Was I erasing everything? Was I making it look too perfect?

I pretty much expected what came next.

"Have you been talking to Sarah?"

The big question I was asked in one form or another every day. It should have been getting easier to lie, but the guilt was starting to pile up, so it only got harder.

"I'm not talking to anyone. I just like my computer clean. It runs faster that way."

Mom looked at me sideways.

"Now we're talking!" Henry yelled. He was balancing some king-size pancakes on a spatula in one hand and carrying a handful of paper plates in the other. My mom kept looking at me, but Henry had saved me from any more cross-examination at the dinner table. She left me alone after that, but I had the feeling she didn't trust me. I couldn't blame her, and was worried it would mean she'd be watching even closer than before. With school starting in only a week, her radar was dialled in and searching for clues.

In another half an hour, it'll be dark. I can't get out of here. If I go for a walk alone, they'll assume I'm trying to see Sarah.

I haven't heard from her all day.

I bet she's sent me something.

The blue rock in the morning — that's the soonest I can try to contact her.

Tuesday, September 21, 8:56 a.m.

As soon as my parents left for work, I crept out the screen door and down the front porch. (Henry snored in the guest room, so getting by him wasn't a problem.) I walked through town, down the main artery of Main Street, passing the twenty side streets that shoot off like veins. It still amazes me that this is our whole town. My house more or less on one end, and Sarah's on the other end, down a street that doesn't look a whole lot different from mine.

I remember when we were seven or eight years old and we spent an entire day trying to figure out the exact halfway point between our houses. We did it because neither of us liked to walk any further than we had to, and we thought it was only fair to split the distance as precisely as possible. After hours of pacing and figuring and drawing a map of the town, we came to the conclusion that the old station house for the train conductor was exactly halfway between our houses. We would sometimes call each other on the phone and then race there. She won every single time. After a while I figured out that she'd tricked me by putting the middle on her side of Main Street, not mine, thereby making it possible for her to use a shortcut we hadn't used when calculating the distance.

I think girls are much craftier than boys when they're little.

In any case, by the time I figured out the whole distance problem, it was too late. We'd decided we needed a marker at our spot.

First we found the rock. It took both of us to move it under the station house and centre it just right.

"Let's paint it," said Sarah.

"Why?" I said.

"Because I want to paint it. Don't you want to paint it?"

"Sure. Let's paint the rock. Why not?"

This very short conversation says a lot about my relationship with Sarah. She wants to do something, I don't necessarily care one way or the other, and so we do it. Eight years later, I have come to discover this is no way to lead a life.

It can get you into a lot of trouble.

It might even get you killed.

It was more out of opportunity than anything else that

the rock became blue. It is the colour of Sarah's house because she stole an old can of paint from her garage. We didn't have a brush, so she just poured the paint over the top like hot fudge on ice cream.

And you know what's funny about this? The paint can is still under there, too.

We didn't know what else to do with it. What if we tossed it in a ditch and someone found it? It was Sarah's House Blue, and someone would tell.

The blue rock became the place we met, where we put secret notes and treasures we'd found and candy we wanted to share.

We were secretive like everyone else in town, even back then. We didn't want anyone hearing us talk about the blue rock. It was ours. And it wasn't easy to find.

The train still comes through town in the early morning, but it never stops here any more. It used to, a long time ago, when the dredge was pounding away 24/7, digging up something worth stopping for. But the old station house was already abandoned when we were kids, so we set about exploring it. It wasn't too intimidating, only about the size of a backyard storage shed on the edge of the tracks. It was locked up tight, but the cool thing was you could climb underneath it. The station house was up off the ground for some reason – I think so it was the same height as the train conductor when he came by – and the cheapest way to accomplish the extra height was to put this little shack on a bunch of cinder blocks. Weeds had grown up all around the edges, sort of like a curtain you could pull back. It was cold gravel underneath, and when we crawled inside, it crunched under our knees.

As we grew older, there wasn't much point in meeting at the blue rock or leaving secret notes there. I hadn't been back there in years. My leg was already tired and sore from the long walk, and the space under the station house seemed a lot smaller than when I was seven. I'd be lucky if I fit at all.

Did I mention that I don't like confined spaces?

I squeezed in on my back and slid under, through the weeds, until I hit my head on the blue rock.

It was a big rock, and I hit it hard enough that I yelled.

Once I recovered, I craned my neck around and saw a piece of paper taped to the rock. I took it, carefully removed the tape, and taped my own note to the slick, blue surface.

The note I had written was short.

Your parents aren't the only ones watching closely. My mom is on my case, too. I think Bonner might have said something to her but I can't tell for sure. She and my dad are very worried about me going back to school — I can tell. I bet they've told all our teachers to keep an eye on us so we don't talk to each other. I hate this!

I'm not sure I even want to go back to school.

Ever.

Too many people in that place.

Being away from you makes everything
feel like it's fading away.
   I should be more afraid, right?
   I hope you sent a video.
   I need to see you.
   Ryan

I read Sarah's note on the walk home. It was easy, since
it was so short. It wasn't even a letter at all. I wish
she'd write me a letter, but Sarah doesn't write if she
can say it in a video.

Hey, Ryan — Miss you / wish I could see you
Password carlkolchak
xoxoxo Sarah

Technically that's not even a note; it's just a handover of some vital information.

No punctuation, unless you count dashes and slashes.

And who's Carl Kolchak?

This is the first time she's used a password I've never heard of.

Anyway, when I got home, I found Henry on the porch eating leftover pancakes with peanut butter.

"You didn't go down there and throw rocks in my favourite fishing hole, did you?" he asked. He seemed genuinely nervous that I'd been up early and scared all the fish out of his number one spot on the creek.

"Just out for a walk is all," I said. "The fish are fine."

He stuffed a big slab of pancake in his mouth and gave me his best comic evil eye as I walked past.

Finally, I got back here to my room, so I could write down these words.

Sarah's at school and I'm stuck here at home.

I already checked out that password online. I'm sort of surprised I didn't catch it, but then again, that show aired before I was born. I can't be expected to know every scary pop culture reference, right?

Still, I had to laugh at that Carl Kolchak. Classic.

I wonder what Sarah found?

SARAHFINCHER.COM
PASSWORD:
CARLKOLCHAK

Tuesday, September 21, 9:17 a.m.

She got me.

I mean she _really_ got me.

I just about had my nose on the screen when that thing went off.

I screamed so loud I think it woke Henry downstairs.

I can hear him moving around in the kitchen.

But it was good — it was OK.

Seeing Sarah laugh was worth it.

That's the part I replayed seven or eight times. Watching her smile like that makes me believe we could get back to where we once were. Before Old Joe Bush and Daryl Bonner. Before I couldn't trust my dad or see my best friend.

I just watched it again.

She's got a great laugh.

Sarah must have sent that video really early this morning while I was sleeping.

Only forty-five minutes and she'll be in the computer lab at school.

I'm getting breakfast.

Tuesday, September 21, 10:21 a.m.

Sarah sent me something sort of scary from school, which I have already watched.

Here's what happened, starting when I left my room an hour ago:

I took my phone downstairs with me and left it in the front pocket of the same hoodie I wore to bed last night. I always leave it set on vibrate instead of sound, and it went off while I was drinking coffee with Henry (unlike my mom, Henry couldn't care less what I drink for breakfast). I couldn't check my phone until I was alone . . . and I couldn't be alone because Henry wanted to play a game of cribbage at the kitchen table.

I was whipping him good, which is hard to do because he's played a lot of cribbage. I couldn't just fold up and leave, so I stayed and finished the game. He came back from thirty pegs behind and beat me in the final hand.

"You lost your concentration right there," said Henry, pointing his finger to the general area where my pegs were sitting when the pocket of my hoodie had started to vibrate.

He didn't know how right he was.

If Sarah had sent me a message, I didn't care about winning, I just wanted the game to be over.

"Better luck next time, champ," said Henry.

I wasn't sure what to make of Sarah's message, which I sneaked a look at once I was free of the kitchen and had started up the stairs.

"Be careful checking that thing," said Henry. "Stairs require the full attention of a one-legged man."

I was startled to hear Henry's voice. He'd obviously followed me out of the kitchen and somehow knew what I was doing. I pocketed my phone and turned all in one motion and saw that Henry had already gone into the guest room. He peeked around the corner and looked up at me where I stood on the second stair.

"I don't care if you talk to her. I think keeping you two apart is about the stupidest thing I've ever heard. I told your dad that."

I was shocked. Did he really know I had a message from Sarah?

"What did he say?"

"Sorry, pal, he's firm as concrete on this. He won't budge. But I won't spy for him. If you want to call Sarah, I won't say a word. I've always liked her."

"Thanks, Henry."

"You owe me one. I'm sure I'll figure out a way to collect before I go."

He went back into his room and started packing some of his things. He'd be gone in a day, and I was sure going to miss him.

I went to my room as fast as I could and shut the door.

She must have seen something to take this kind of risk. No message, no note, nothing — just three words run together on my phone. imatschool

I figured that must be the password — imatschool — so I jumped online and went straight to Sarah's site.

What I saw there made me realize something important.

Something big was about to happen.

SARAHFINCHER.COM
PASSWORD:
IMATSCHOOL

Tuesday, September 21, 11:00 a.m.

I knew it! Mr Bramson never watches us in the computer lab. Never. He's practically nonexistent because we run these tutorials that tell us how to use Microsoft Excel or Word or some other evil empire program. Mr Bramson types away on his own computer, which sits on the corner of his desk. He's probably sending emails or reading news headlines. He doesn't even look up unless someone asks him a question, which is basically _never_.

So why is Mr Bramson watching Sarah? I'll tell you why — because my parents have told him to. Mr Bramson is spying on us!

I knew they were ruthless, but seriously — my parents telling our teachers to make sure we're not talking to each other? They've gone even further than I thought they would. Do they really think Sarah and I are that dangerous together? I mean, what do they _really_ think? We're going to get into deadly trouble or something?

Fine.

If it's deadly trouble they want, then deadly trouble they're going to get.

Breaking and entering? Check.

Planting secret cameras at a meeting for a society that appears to be killing people left and right? Check.

Seeing Sarah as much as I want? Check! Check! Check!

I don't even care any more.

Tuesday, September 21, 2:00 p.m.

I've calmed down a little bit, but I'm still mad.
I went for a long walk.
I don't feel like writing.

Tuesday, September 21, 10:00 p.m.

I sat through dinner and said almost nothing.

Henry leaves tomorrow, so I felt sort of bad.

But I couldn't even look at my parents.

They think they're so sneaky.

Right in the middle of dinner, Dad excuses himself to use the bathroom.

There's a perfectly good bathroom downstairs, but he goes upstairs and uses the one up there. Or so he says.

I know what he's doing.

He's in my room, checking my computer.

Searching the drawers.

Looking under my bed for journals or notes.

Staring out the window and wondering — what's this kid up to?

Well, good luck, Dad. You're not going to find anything. You know why? Because I'm sneakier than you by a long shot. I got this wonderful trait from you, Mr Secret Society. You passed it down and it got bigger and better. You're an amateur with your wooden bird and flushing the toilet like you think I'm actually going to believe you're using the bathroom up there.

Afterward, I went straight to my room and wrote a huge, complicated, get-in-the-worst-kind-of-trouble email to Sarah.

Hi, Sarah. I hope you got my note at the blue rock. It was a real trick getting under there. I hit my head. I have a feeling you knew how hard that delivery would be for me and chose the blue rock to exchange notes anyway. Hey, if it puts a smile on your face, I'm happy.

Speaking of smiling, you were doing a lot of that when you tricked me with that Carl Kolchak video. Pop culture reference from 80s TV = Sarah is about to play a trick, dead ahead. I should have known. Next time I won't be such an easy target.

Okay – the good news – are you ready? I know how to get inside Longhorn's in the middle of the night when it's closed up.

I've spent a lot of time in that place because Dad runs the fly-fisherman's club. I know you know about the club, but I'm not sure you've ever been aware of how often I associate with this group of misfit fishing bums. I don't talk about it because it seems the slightest bit nerdy to be heading down to Longhorn's every Thursday night to tie flies and talk about trout with old guys. At least it comes in handy now, right?

Here's how you get yourself in there after hours:

There is a window in the men's room – I know it's not painted shut because I checked it once just to see for myself. Longhorn's Grange is open on weekdays for all kinds of things, like on Tuesdays when the old ladies meet up and sew quilts in there. And no, I'm not part of the blanket-making club. My grandma was before she died, so that's how I know. I've got a fishing-themed quilt on my bed to prove it.

I think I could get in there tomorrow during the day and unlatch that window. The only way to reach it is from the top of the sink, but my leg is feeling better every day and I'm sure I can do this. Tomorrow night, if you go to the bathroom side of Longhorn's, you should be able to pull that window open and climb inside.

Bring a ladder. The window is pretty high.

Okay, second thing (did I mention that it's getting late and I'm tired – I hope I can stay awake long enough to finish this monster email). Second thing is. . .

The black door on the stage.

Years ago – this must have been when I was first attending the fly-fishing club with my dad – I wandered off from my tying vice and got up on the stage. The amps were there for the bands when they have dances, and I was turning the knobs this way and that. There's a drum set on the stage, too. They just leave it there because it's so hard to move, I guess.

So I started tap-tap-tapping on this drum set and my dad hollered at me.

I stopped.

That was when I saw the black door.

Tuesday, September 21, Midnight

I fell asleep at my desk.

This is bad.

Really bad.

I didn't finish the email to Sarah.

The screen is black on my laptop. It went to sleep a few minutes after I did, so the screen went dim, but I can't be sure that nobody came in here and saw it. All you have to do is wipe your hand across the mouse and the screen comes back on, big and bright, and I'm in huge trouble.

I moved the mouse and it came back up right where I left off.

<u>That was when I saw the black door.</u>

I remember what happened.

I took a break and leaned back in my chair.

I rubbed my leg because it felt like it was falling asleep.

I had turned the light off so it was totally dark except for the light from my screen.

I leaned forward again, placed my elbow on my desk, and rested my head on my hand.

That's the last thing I remember.

A couple of minutes later the screen must've gone dark.

I woke up and it was pitch-black in my room and I decided right then and there that falling asleep was just the beginning of my problems.

The real problem was what woke me up.

Old Joe Bush.

He was in my room. I'm sure of it.

I heard him.

I heard the leg dragging down the hallway.

I didn't dream it! I know I didn't dream it.

You want to know how I know I didn't dream it?

Because I did something then. Something I should not have done. By the light of my computer monitor I crept over to the *Dark Side of the Moon* poster. The one that covered the words on my wall.

<u>Don't make me come looking for you.</u>

I lifted the poster out of the way from the bottom. The tape wasn't very sticky, so it was easy. My shadow covered the wall and I couldn't see the words, so I moved to the side.

And there they were.

More words.

Words that hadn't been there before.

The Apostle will see you now.

I taped the poster down and came back to my desk.

Did I write those words or did he?

I don't remember having the pen in my hand.

And I don't think it's my handwriting.

Either I wrote both messages or I didn't write either one.

And what does this new message even mean?

The Apostle will see you now.

He's watching me.

It means I stepped over the line and I'm next. The Apostle is dead. I'm dead.

I feel a chill that runs right down the centre of my broken leg, like it's in the freezer and it's about to crack into a thousand pieces from the cold. That kind of feeling doesn't come from nowhere.

I don't think it's a feeling from this world. It's from The Apostle's world, Joe Bush's world — it's from the kingdom of the dead.

I'm just about sure he was here.

Either that or I'm going crazy.

I sent the email to Sarah unfinished just to get it off my screen.

I can't tell her this stuff. I can't. It's not like being a member of my dad's fishing club. This is different. She'll think I've lost it. She won't trust me any more.

I started a new email.

Sarah — You have to turn bolts on three sides to release the black door, so bring a flat-blade screwdriver with you. Once you get it open, you'll see the stairs going down.

I'll make sure the window is open so you can get in. I'm sure you've got a plan for how to run the camera. You always do.

Gotta go – miss you. Ryan

I took a close-up picture of my wall and printed it out at my desk.

Having a picture of it makes the words real.

I'm not making this up. I'm not seeing things.

Wednesday, September 22, 1:00 a.m.

I can't sleep.

Wednesday, September 22, 2:00 a.m.

I can't sleep.

Wednesday, September 22, 3:00 a.m.

I won't sleep.
I'm not writing on these walls.
It's someone else.

Wednesday, September 22, 5:00 a.m.

I zonked out for a couple of hours. Then, when I woke up, I refused to look behind that poster again.

Sarah emailed me, pretty upset. She wasn't too keen on the long email after we agreed not to take chances. But then she said it was nearly impossible _not_ to email each other. She was doing it, too. Just be careful, she said — erase, erase, erase. Leave no trace. Our relationship doesn't exist.

I hate the sound of that.

Our relationship doesn't exist.

Have my parents won?

Sarah's email went on and got a little better. Talk about breaking her own rules. I've almost never seen her write this much. Maybe she misses me after all.

I think your idea with the window at Longhorn's is perfect. No one's up there at night, especially around that back side in the weeds, so it should work. I can already imagine the questions if Bonner catches me walking up the street with a ladder at midnight. That's not even something I want to think about. Let's see – 4 a.m. right now. I've been getting by on almost no sleep lately. I think the detective in me thinks early morning is the safest time or something – either way, I'm wide awake, so I'll haul one of my dad's old ladders up there in the next hour and hide it in the brush behind Longhorn's. Not that anyone is going behind Longhorn's to find it.

I have a feeling that crow is going to move again soon. Crossbones members probably check it every day, right? If that's true, then it sure would be nice to watch and see who takes a particular interest in it today. Or maybe we could see someone actually moving the birdie – wouldn't that be something? If we knew who that was, we'd be one step closer.

I need you to do something for me. There's a perfect spot downtown at the café. If you sit at the corner table, there's a nice view of the library right across the street. Just go in there with your journal or something and tell them you had to get out of the house. Marla won't care. She knows your mom, so I'm sure she'll be happy you're out of the house. Just sit there and drink coffee and eat pie and scribble.

I think someone will move the signal while I'm at school. There are only a few days before they burn down the dredge. Whoever is in the Crossbones can't wait much longer. They're just as interested in the dredge as we are – we just don't know why. And Gladys knows I'm snooping around. So does Bonner. They're watching me as much as I'm watching them. I think they'll move it while I'm at school so I can't see it happen.

Let's try to be as safe as we can. Every one of these emails is an invitation to get caught. Leave me a note at the blue rock and let me know what you find out. I'll stop there on my way home and check. If it's anything interesting, I'll leave you a note on the rock and we'll go from there. Sorry to send you running around, but if we're as close to some sort of Crossbones event as I think we are, we need to be extra careful.

Hang in there. Have a slice of pie for me.

Delete! Delete! Delete!

Sarah

I'm actually sort of excited about getting out of my room.
I don't like it in here any more.

Wednesday, September 22, 10:00 a.m.

I'm sitting at the café all by myself. I just got here.

Right after I deleted Sarah's email, I went back to bed. The sun was coming up, which made me feel safer. That whole vampire thing is so right on. Darkness and evil go together like sprinkles on cupcakes. It's amazing how much calmer I am when it's light.

Anyway, I didn't wake up until an hour ago, and then I went downstairs and discovered that my dad had decided to stay home from work and spend the day with Henry. He (Henry) is leaving tomorrow. My dad took all of last week off from work. He was supposed to take this week off, too, but, according to him, "the place was falling apart." My dad has worked for the same company since before I was born. He's a maintenance mechanic at a paper mill, which means he works on a gigantic metal machine with a lot of moving parts. The machine is worth a lot of money. If it breaks down, it's a big deal. The problem is my dad has been there so long everyone else is younger or less experienced than he is with this dinosaur of a machine. So if it rattles or shakes funny, everyone freaks out and they call my dad.

"It's amazing they lasted a week," he said when I was down on the porch. "Took two days just to calm everyone down. But I still have time for a Cabela's run."

Yes, Dad had that sporting goods gleam in his eye. I mean, at Cabela's, the fishing section alone is bigger than some of the lakes I've been on.

"You should come with us," said Henry. He was wearing a cowboy hat I hadn't seen before.

"Where'd you get that hat?" I asked.

Henry took it off and examined it with some pride.

"Yard sale. Two bucks. Can you believe that?"

"Did you wash it?"

Henry looked at the cowboy hat as if he hadn't thought of that but probably should have, then he set it on his knee and looked back at me for an answer about whether or not I was going with them.

"I'm not sure I can walk that much," I lied. A trip to Cabela's sounded amazing and I totally could have done it. "But I might walk downtown and back."

My dad piped in. "I'm glad to hear you're at least thinking of getting outside. That room of yours is starting to smell funny."

The truth is — and this was actually OK with me — I could tell my dad wanted a few hours alone with his best friend on his last day in town. I could understand how important it was even if he didn't.

"You guys have a good time," I said. "Don't spend too much of my college fund."

I knew as well as my dad did how easy it was to blow months of savings at Cabela's in a matter of hours.

Dad's timing seemed to be working out really well for me, since I was supposed to be watching the crow all day from the vantage point of the café. But then Henry went inside to run a dishrag around the rim of his new cowboy hat, and my dad and I were left alone on the porch. He sipped his coffee and set the cup on a folding card table that had seen more action on the front porch in the past week than it had in the previous year.

"How's that leg doing? You ready for school?" he asked.

He didn't sound like he was going to badger me about Sarah, so I played along.

"I think I'll be OK. Seeing some of my friends will be nice. It's getting a little old being home every day."

"I'm glad to hear it. Sitting around Skeleton Creek will get you nowhere."

He picked up his cup and looked at the drawing on the side. My dad is very fond of a good coffee cup, and this one, I had to admit, was my favourite.

It was white, with an old *Far Side* cartoon on it where two deer are standing together and one of them has a big red bull's-eye on its chest. The one without the bull's-eye looks at this poor deer and says, "Bummer of a birthmark."

I was thinking how clever this was when my dad said, "Let me see your phone."

He knew I kept it with me a lot of the time and there was no point trying to hide the fact that I had it just then, so I gave it to him.

He had become a lot savvier with phones and computers in the past few weeks. The accident seemed to wake him up to the fact that he needed to know what was going on or risk missing something that might get me killed. In a weird way this made me feel loved, like he was willing to put in some effort in order to protect me from myself.

But like I've been saying all along, I'm two steps ahead of my dad when it comes to stuff like this. Every teenager is. Most parents, even ones like mine that are actually trying to keep up, are perpetually behind.

He touched some of the buttons — obviously checking it for text messages from Sarah and callback numbers. I'd had plenty of calls from other friends I wasn't close to but stayed in contact with anyway. But he wasn't going to find anything from Sarah.

I was surprised when he held the phone to his ear. He was using my phone to call someone. No one answered, so he hung up and handed the phone back to me.

"No one's home at Sarah's," he said.

If she had been there, she would have picked up. Caller ID would have told her it was my mobile phone. It's a lucky thing she was gone.

He dug into his back pocket and pulled out a fat wallet. This is one of the old-school things I like about my dad. I love his old jeans and the prehistoric leather belt that holds them up, but this wallet — I don't know, it seems like the sort of thing I'd never carry. It's shaped funny, like it's been sat on for twenty years. Its worn leather is dark in the middle and lighter on the edges. And when my dad opens it up, there are all kinds of treasures in there. Pieces of paper from I don't know where, notes about forgotten things, faded pictures of me and Mom, pennies and nickels that have left round marks in the leather.

"Here," he said, handing me a twenty with a fold in one corner. "Get yourself a new shirt while you're downtown. Might come in handy for school."

Henry burst out on to the porch with the hat back on his head, all excited about getting on the road. He wanted to be back before two o'clock so they could fish the creek one last time. Dad finished his coffee, and soon they were gone in my dad's pickup, leaving the house empty except for me. I stayed on the porch, afraid to go up the stairs to my room.

I was starting to hate my room.

I finally got up the nerve to enter the house. It should have been no big deal climbing the stairs, but I took it real slow and quiet, like something bad might happen if I was too loud.

Slowly I headed up the stairs, cursing every creaky step until I reached the top. I looked down the hall and thought about searching my dad's room again. But I didn't have the guts to do it. Once was enough.

I gathered a couple of journals, some pens, and a copy of Edgar Allan Poe's best short stories. I felt in my pocket for the twenty my dad had handed me.

That, I figured, should buy plenty of pie and coffee.

Wednesday, September 22, 11:30 a.m.

The waitress my mom knows isn't working today, which has led me to consume more cups of coffee than should be allowed by law. My hands are shaking. I can feel my heart racing in my chest. This can't be good for me.

Two slices of pie couldn't have helped. That's a lot of sugar. But I can't drink coffee on an empty stomach.

I've got ten bucks left.

How much am I supposed to tip this lady?

She keeps asking me if I want a refill and I keep saying yes so I'll have a reason to stay without seeming like I'm just taking up space.

How does one become a waitress in a dead-end town? I've never seen her around here before. I'd guess she's about twenty-five. Did she move here? And, if so, what the heck for?

She probably married a local who moved back here. She couldn't have known what she was getting herself into.

Bummer for her.

From where I'm sitting I can see the library, but the black crow above the door is at an angle and too far away. To my eyes, it's an indistinct blob of black above the door. I've been scouting the angle, though, and it looks to me like Dr Watts could see the crow from the second story of his house. He's only a half block off Main Street, and his window points in the right direction.

I haven't seen anyone enter or leave the library all morning. Not even Gladys, who, I assume, is holed up inside, either reading something hugely boring or concocting some sort of scheme to get me killed. I think now is my best chance to get inside the men's room at Longhorn's. I can't remember what happens there on Wednesdays, but something is always going on in the middle of the day. I don't think it's the quilt-making club and I know it's not fly-tying.

My plan is to do this quickly and get back so I don't miss it if the crow gets moved. I want to see who does it. So I'll swing past Dr Watts's house and see if he really can catch a glimpse of the front of the library, and then I'll go to Longhorn's and return here. I should be able to do all that in an hour. Maybe faster with this caffeine jump in my step.

Wednesday, September 22, 12:43 p.m.

That took longer than I expected. How was I supposed to know they were building trains up at Longhorn's? Have you ever stumbled into a room full of model train enthusiasts? Those guys are big-time recruiters, so they wouldn't leave me alone. They'd all heard about my accident and some old-timer told this really horrible story about a conductor who fell between two train cars and held on for dear life with both hands. His legs bounced around until finally someone found him and hauled him back to safety, but by that time both his legs were broken.

So then this guy says to me, "Lucky he didn't end up under the train. That's a whole 'nother story you don't even want to hear."

I hadn't wanted to hear the first story, either, but that hadn't stopped him from telling it to me, and sure enough he told me this other story about the guy who fell under the train. I'm not going to repeat it. It's a bad story.

Once they had me standing there, I had to hear about the engines and the trains that used to run through town and look at all their models and on and on. It was pretty interesting, actually. I was standing there thinking, Hey, I could join these guys if I didn't have school. I could get my own train and do some research on this and that. These old guys aren't that bad.

In other words, I was distracted.

It was about thirty minutes after I'd left the café that I realized I was away from my post and was probably missing Old Joe Bush himself turning the black crow on the steps of the library.

I excused myself to use the men's room.

Once I was in there, I realized a sink is a lot easier to climb on top of when you don't have a leg that was recently broken into a bunch of pieces. But I was determined to get that window open for Sarah. I must have been in there a long time, like ten minutes, because I had only just unlatched the top window and got halfway down again when I heard someone at the door peeking in, asking if I was OK, had I fallen into the toilet — the usual stuff.

I sort of half fell, half climbed the rest of the way down and landed on my rear end on the tile floor. It's a miracle I didn't hurt myself. The same guy who had told me the two train stories helped me up and tried to make me feel better by commenting on how difficult it must be to go to the bathroom with a broken leg, etc., etc.

The funny thing was, I'd had about ten cups of coffee and I <u>really</u> needed to use the bathroom. But I'd already been in there for ever so I made for the door and headed back here, to the café, which is where I'm sitting.

I went straight to the bathroom.

When I got back, there was a glass of water at my table. (<u>My table</u> — how funny is that? I never come in here.)

"More coffee?" the waitress asked me. She said it like she'd prefer it if I found somewhere else to take up space on the planet. We'd been sharing idle chit-chat all morning about school, my injury, the town, but generally she was a one- or two-word conversationalist and this "More coffee?" question was all I was going to get.

"Can I just stick with the water instead?" I asked.

She gave me the evil eye, like I was a freeloader, so I ordered a third slice of pie... and kept my eye on the crow.

It still hasn't changed.

Wednesday, September 22, 12:58 p.m.

I can't believe what just happened.

Ten or fifteen minutes ago while I'm choking down a bite of cherry pie, guess who I see coming up Main Street—

Our friendly neighbourhood park ranger. Daryl Bonner.

He walked right past the library, glanced at it, and crossed the street.

I slumped behind my journal and then thought I better not have it out or he might turn private eye on me and try to confiscate it as evidence. Can a park ranger do that? I don't know, but he's got a uniform and he's a big guy, so I didn't take any chances. I bent down and put it in my backpack, and when I glanced back up again, I heard the bell ding at the café door and watched Ranger Bonner walk towards my table.

I'm not sure if it was all the coffee I'd drunk or what, but I was super nervous.

"Hi, Ranger Bonner," I said with this shaky voice. It sounded like I'd just thrown someone under a train.

The rest of the conversation went like this:

Bonner: "Feeling better, I see."

Me: "Yes, much. Thank you, sir."

Bonner: "Seen Sarah lately?"

Me: "No, sir. I haven't seen her in a long time."

Bonner: "You know, she's still snooping around. She can't seem to leave things alone."

Me: "I wasn't aware, since I haven't seen her."

(Mind you, my voice was shaking every time I opened my mouth. No more coffee!)

Bonner: "You're sure you haven't talked to her?"

Me: "Oh, I'm sure. I'd remember that."

Bonner: "Very funny."

Me: "Not trying to be funny, sir."

He looked at me sideways and stood up. I could tell he didn't trust me.

That's all we need — Daryl Bonner following me and Sarah.

He made for the door without turning back, then disappeared down the block.

I drank a glass of water, went to the bathroom again, and stared at the library.

Sitting at the café was making me realize I don't want to be a spy when I grow up. Too much sitting around doing nothing.

Five more minutes just went by and I'm...

Oh, no. Don't tell me. This can't be.

Is that...

...my dad?

He's coming up Main on the other side of the street.

What time is it?

1:05 p.m.

He and Henry are back from the city like they said. But they should be heading for the creek.

OK, I'm just going to slide down in this booth, watch him, and take a few notes.

He's in front of the library.

Looking both ways.

Now looking off towards Dr Watts's house.

He's going up the steps.

Has his hand on the crow.

I can't see what he's doing!

He's down the steps and crossing the street.

Coming towards me?

He can't come in here. No way!

Here he is, right in front of the window, about to reach the door.

Hold your breath, Ryan — that always helps.

Keep your head down. Keep writing.

He's walking like he's got somewhere to be.

He's gone down the street, towards my house and out of sight.

That was way too close. If he saw me watching him, I don't know what I'd do.

Or what he'd do.

I can't see the crow. I should have brought binoculars!

Hold on. Something else is happening.

Wednesday, September 22, 2:19 p.m.

OK, the past hour has been a whirlwind, but I'll try to explain fast. I couldn't go back to the café or I'm sure that waitress would have been like, "What is your problem?"

I can't take that kind of stress right now.

So I'm sitting at the station house. Not under the station house, with the blue rock, but on the steps leading up to the door that's never unlocked.

I wonder what's in there?

<u>Scatterbrain!!!!</u>

I need someone to slap me so I can calm down.

So here's what happened in the past hour:

I packed up my stuff and left the café. I've never walked around in our tiny, hanging-on-for-its-life downtown with so much anxiety. I've never worried about who might be watching me. My dad could be right around the corner. Daryl Bonner might be staring out from behind a window. Gladys Morgan could come out at any moment and point her shotgun at me. And that Dr Watts guy — he might have his binoculars trained on me, call some thug on his phone, and they'd find me wrapped around a tree in the creek tomorrow morning.

I turned down a side street as soon as I was outside the café and walked away from the library, towards the woods. There are woods all around Skeleton Creek, but the café was on the side of the street opposite the big mountains. I glanced up at them and saw how small the library was in their monstrous shadow. All those books don't add up to a hill of beans against one big mountain. I turned down a side alley and couldn't stop thinking about a pile of books — like every book ever printed — and I wondered if all those books would be as big as the one mountain. Makes a guy wonder about who made mountains and why they were made so big.

So all these thoughts were running through my head, which kept me from being too nervous at the thought of turning a corner into my dad or Ranger Bonner or Gladys ready to slap me across the face with a copy of War and Peace or Lord of the Rings. Before I knew it, I was walking past the library, glancing up at the black crow as my throat tightened. It was a very quick glance, like reading a clock and going back to my homework, but that was all the time I needed to see that my dad had changed the time.

<u>A straight shot to Martha's at ten past the knob.</u>

<u>A straight shot to Martha's at ten past the knob.</u>
<u>A straight shot to Martha's at ten past the knob.</u>

I kept repeating those words because I'd memorized them from The Alchemist Diagram of 79.

Before I knew how I even got there, I was across the street, down a block, and sitting on the kerb, shaking uncontrollably. I thought about the mountain of books and my body not growing. I breathed the mountain air in and out until I felt a little better. It dawned on me then that I should keep watching from where I sat. No one had seen me — or at least if they had, they hadn't stopped me. Maybe something else would happen. I stood and peeked around the corner on to Main Street. I sort of leaned on the brick building like I was playing it cool in case anyone walked past.

I waited.

Five minutes went by. 1:51.

Five more minutes passed. 1:56.

People walked by the library, but no one appeared to look at the crow. No one went inside the library. It just sat there until 1:58, when Gladys Morgan opened the door and came outside. She stood there for a moment looking up and down Main Street.

Then she looked at me.

I didn't move, and it wasn't because I wanted her to see me. I just <u>couldn't</u> move.

She stared right at me and I half expected to hear her whisper, "Don't make me come looking for you."

But she acted like she hadn't seen me at all. Gladys is ancient, so I was likely nothing more than a cataract-induced blob next to a fuzzy building. Still, it was creepy the way she stopped and held her gaze right where I was standing, like she knew someone was hiding just outside her ability to see.

Gladys turned around, looked at the black crow, and went back into the library.

2:00 p.m.

I lingered.

I don't even know for sure why. It wasn't like I had it all figured out or anything, but something told me to stay. This little dance wasn't done yet.

At 2:03 p.m., my dad came back.

He walked casually up the pavement and jumped the two steps to the library door.

He didn't see me.

I watched him reach up and move the crow, and

when he did, I realized he was doing the job The Apostle had once done.

The Apostle will see you now.

Could my dad have written those words?

If he did, he's crazy. Meet my dad, escapee from the nuthouse.

Or was it worse than crazy?

Was it deadly?

No. I couldn't think about that.

He would've been just a kid when Joe Bush died.

A kid like me.

I walked to the blue rock so I could leave a note for Sarah. Now here I sit with the sun beating down on my head. Stress makes you do things you shouldn't. It's that whole fight-or-flight thing. I worked my leg way too hard today without even realizing I was doing it. It didn't hurt then, but it hurts a lot now.

I hope I haven't re-injured it.

I'm not looking forward to the long walk back home.

The lies I'll have to tell about what I've been doing all day.

The questions about the shirt I didn't buy with the money my dad gave me.

But wait – who's the real liar here?

My dad moved the signal, then moved it back.

Everyone in the Crossbones knew they were supposed to look between 1 p.m. and 2 p.m. on Wednesday. Maybe they've been looking for years. Who knows? Probably it's all part of some elaborate system. The crow moves the first time and everyone knows it will move again at 1 p.m. the next day? Could be. That would make sense, because my dad is gone all day every day. But Dr Watts and Gladys? They're right here. Maybe Dr Watts goes to his top window every day, points his binoculars at the library, and then goes back to whatever it is he does in that old house of his. All Gladys has to do is glance out the door she steps through every day.

Sarah – you're going to have to move fast. Crossbones is meeting below Longhorn's at 12:10 tonight.

I can't walk out here again. My leg is killing me.

You'll have to email me, but my guess is they'll be watching even closer. Send me a note at exactly 9:00 p.m. and let me know if you need me to do anything.

I'll turn in early, tell them I'm tired and not feeling well, and maybe they'll leave me alone.

At least I know my dad won't be home tonight.

My best guess about who you're going to see at this secret meeting? Dr Watts, my dad, Gladys Morgan, and maybe Daryl Bonner.

Everyone else who might have shown up is already dead.

Ryan

Wednesday, September 22, 5:05 p.m.

Sarah is going to email me in a few hours, but right now I'm sitting on the front porch, trying to play it cool. The old couch is getting some holes, but it's the most comfortable place to rest, outside my own room. I hope my mom doesn't move it to the yard and try to sell it.

Dad and Henry are still at the creek fishing, which doesn't surprise me. Some of the best bugs come out in the late afternoon and early evening. They might not be back until 7:00 or 8:00, especially if they're trying to avoid another dinner like last night. I've had the house to myself all afternoon and Mom won't be home for another hour. I brought my laptop downstairs at three, and for the past two hours I've been digging around.

Three cans of Coke later, I've found some amazing stuff.

I have decided that I'm obsessed with Robert Boyle, Robert Hooke, and Sir Isaac Newton. As far as I'm concerned, these guys were rock stars. I can see how a secret society would be interested in them. Who doesn't love a mad scientist? But after the research I did today, I think I'm starting to see a bigger reason why the members of the Crossbones have been interested in Boyle, Hooke and Newton.

A brief history of these three people is worth writing down. First Hooke. Robert Hooke.

Many historians believe Hooke was the first person to use the word <u>cell</u> in relation to biology. That alone makes him larger than life. Imagine being the first person to use the word <u>pizza</u> or <u>football</u> or <u>movie</u>. Those are nothing compared to the word for the building block of all life as we know it (including pizza, footballs and movies). Impressive.

Robert Hooke did all these experiments with air pumps and springs and elastic — a bunch of really great stuff. A lot of people give Hooke credit for inventing the balance spring, which is what makes small timepieces possible. He theorized correctly about combustion decades before anyone else understood it. He invented barometers, optical devices, microscopes and universal joints. Hooke was one of the first people to accurately measure weather, to see objects too tiny for the naked eye, and survey huge parts of London so it could be rebuilt after the great fire of 1666. (He also figured out some very important stuff about elasticity, but I have to admit I don't really understand it.)

One of Sir Isaac Newton's most famous lines was actually in a letter he wrote to Robert Hooke:

<u>If I have seen further it is by standing on the shoulders of giants</u>.

So that's what Sir Isaac Newton, the discoverer of <u>gravity</u>, thought of Hooke. Not bad.

Sir Isaac Newton is even more important than I realized. Sure, I knew he was impressive, but I could have spent all day researching the things he invented and discovered and not even scratched the surface.

From gravity to planetary movements, from calculus to how light works, Newton was at the forefront of so many ground-breaking discoveries it's no wonder he is known as the father of science.

And then there was the last of the three, Robert Boyle, who turns out to be the most interesting.

Let's start with his hair.

The guy had guts to go out on the streets of London looking like that. Wow. Plenty of wigs to choose from at the wig shop and he chose the biggest of the bunch.

Robert Boyle was a scientist with devout religious beliefs. After reading up on him, I think this was one of the key things that made Boyle unique. It's not that other notable scientists of his time had no faith, it's just that Boyle was a Christian first and a scientist second. The fact that he was highly successful at both made him a powerful figure of the times. He admired God's workmanship and saw the study of natural science as a form of worship. The only way, in his view, to discover the world God made was to investigate it. This seems like a sound idea to me.

As far as I can tell, he was a little bit of a nutty professor. Just about everything Boyle ever wrote was short on organization and long on ideas. I imagine, if he'd had a car, the keys would have gone missing all the time. He was constantly refuting the ideas of other chemists and scientists, and although he was often right, this might have had the effect of making him seem like a know-it-all to some.

He was outrageously wealthy, primarily because his

father was one of the richest men in Ireland. His title (I'm not making this up) was the Great Earl of Cork, but I don't think he made corks or pluggers or bottle caps. He lived in Cork, which I guess is a place in Ireland. Anyway, this meant Boyle could afford to hire assistants, including Robert Hooke — yes, that Robert Hooke — to work for him. It was Boyle's idea to explore gases and pumps, but Hooke did many of the hands-on experiments.

Many people regard Robert Boyle as the most important chemist of his time, which makes the fact that he was an alchemist all the more interesting. You heard me right — Robert Boyle, *the* Robert Boyle, was a closet alchemist! And not just a hobby alchemist — he was fairly obsessed with it. Apparently, Sir Isaac Newton also thought a lot about alchemy, but it was Boyle who appears to have been at the forefront of this very subjective science. And while it's harder to find references to Robert Hooke and alchemy, something tells me all three of them were secretly working in this area together.

Alchemy, I'm starting to learn, was then and continues to be today a controversial offshoot of "real chemistry". During Boyle's time, it was viewed as voodoo chemistry where chemicals and metals were brought together in strange ways to accomplish outlandish things. It was not "serious" science.

And here we come to the most interesting thing of all, the thing that makes the appearance of their names in the Crossbones make all the sense in the world.

Robert Boyle wrote a secret paper that didn't surface until long after his death. It was never meant to be published, but it was.

This is what the paper was called:

<u>An Historical Account of a Degradation of Gold Made by an Anti-Elixir.</u>

If you believe this secret paper by Boyle, he was very close to figuring something out — something remarkable and kind of scary for what it could mean. Robert Boyle was very close to finding a way to turn gold into something else.

Imagine if you could change the properties of gold so it wasn't gold any more, and then change it back again. Imagine!

What if you worked on a gold dredge and had a way to hide gold or change gold, then change it back?

It can't be possible, can it? Could Boyle and Hooke and Newton have secretly figured this out, but told no one? What if the secret is out there and someone from my little town figured it out? A process like that sure would come in handy on a gold dredge.

It might start to answer why so many members of the Crossbones ended up dead and why at least one of the dead doesn't want to leave the dredge.

Wednesday, September 22, 9:05 p.m.

I'm stuck in my room, where I just watched the last tiny speck of light from the sun disappear. Summer is fading fast. It used to stay light until almost ten out here.

Not any more.

Mom came home at 6:00 and made me dinner. It wasn't as bad as I expected it to be. But then again, it's hard to mess up when you're making spaghetti and the sauce is out of a jar.

We sat together at the kitchen table and waited for Dad and Henry to come home.

"They're not coming back for dinner, are they?" Mom asked me. She was twirling a fork full of pasta.

"I wouldn't count on it."

Without Henry around, it was quieter. I'm beginning to think I prefer quiet. It's a lot of work, holding up my end of the conversation. Mom and I mostly sat in silence, which was OK. We talked about what I'd done all day and I told her I spent most of it at the café writing and drawing.

"That sounds nice."

"It felt good to be out of the house," I said. "I think

I'm ready to get back to school. This town is awfully dull during the day with no one around."

Mom smiled. I was glad to make her think I wanted to go back to school like a normal kid, even if I wasn't too sure about it myself. There's going to be a lot of questions about the accident and what I've been doing. I could live without all the attention.

Dad and Henry finally stumbled in around 8:00, arguing about who caught the bigger fish and smelling like two guys who hadn't taken a shower in about a month.

"We're starved. What's cooking?" asked Henry.

"Whatever _was_ cooking is gone," Mom replied. "You're on your own."

Henry and my dad looked at each other, shrugged their shoulders, and went straight for the pancake mix.

"What is it with you two and pancakes?" asked my mom.

They didn't answer. Two old friends in the kitchen making the easiest of all foods. I envied them their time together like never before.

"I was out a lot today, and I'm tired," I said.

I didn't mean for it to sound like I was irritated, especially with Henry leaving and all, but I think it was obvious I saw them as a little club no one else was invited into.

"You sure you don't want a cake or two?" Henry said. "I could tell you about how I caught ten times more fish than your dad did."

"I thought you had to go visit Gerald down the road," Dad said.

Henry nodded, but then said, "Gerald can wait a while. He'll be up late. Always is."

Gerald is another old friend of Henry's. He lives in the next town over — a town that has the distinction of having been the very last place in America to get phone service. It's even more of a dead end than Skeleton Creek. Gerald is quite a bit older and can't go fishing any more, but Henry always visits him at least once on every trip out from New York. The fishing had been so good all week he'd put it off until the last minute.

Henry did a little more begging and Dad nodded like he wanted to spend some time with me. So I sat with them on the porch for almost an hour, acting more and more tired as the minutes passed, until Henry jumped out of his chair so he could drive the ten miles down to Gerald's place. I was sure my mom used the time I was on the porch to check my computer and my phone. At least I could turn in early and they wouldn't have any reason to bother me.

I came up here a little while ago, right before the sun started setting, and right at 9:00 I checked my email. Nothing. I checked again at 9:01 and there it was, a note from Sarah. It was cool to think she was sitting at her computer and me at mine, and somehow in those sixty seconds we'd made a connection. She clicked send, I refreshed my screen, and there was the note. It was sort of like magic, and I missed her more than ever.

I'm so glad you stayed at the café! Who knows what would have happened right under our noses if not for you. This is it, Ryan — something really big is happening tonight. And we're going to see it!

I'm sure I can get into the Watts place while the meeting is going on.

My parents, believe it or not, are out on a date. They should be back in about half an hour. I'll see them when they come home so they think everything is all normal. If all goes well, they'll be asleep by eleven and I'll go straight to Longhorn's, then to Dr Watts's house. Watts has to be hiding something, and this is our best chance to find out what. He can't be in two places at once, so we know he'll be out of his house. I just hope I can get inside.

The tape in the camera at Longhorn's Grange will run for about ninety minutes. Hopefully that will be long enough to catch the entire meeting. I'll start it as close to midnight as possible.

Okay – best part of all – I'll broadcast everything live for you. I can't go live with the Crossbones meeting, but I can use my other camera – the one we used to broadcast live in the dredge – to send you a feed. Go to the site at 11:30 p.m. if you can. That's when I'll start broadcasting off and on. Just be sure no one else is watching.

To get into the feed, go to my site and use the password: maryshelley.

Scared but excited! This is going to be incredible!

Sarah

I'm scared for her.
    I mean <u>really</u> scared.
    I'm not sure we should do this.

Wednesday, September 22, 11:10 p.m.

I'm really close to bailing out. This is starting to remind me of the night I left for the dredge and ended up trapped inside the secret room.

I hate the way this feels, like I have no control over things.

All I can do is watch while my best friend breaks into two places in one night.

And what if she gets caught? It's not hard to imagine an alarm on Dr Watts's door going off, or her getting trapped in the basement at Longhorn's Grange. One of those things could easily happen.

I won't be able to do anything but sit here and watch it happen.

I picked up my copy of *Frankenstein* and started reading it to pass the time.

I'm amazed at how much I underlined and took notes in this old paperback. The margins are filled with little questions and comments. I've dog-eared about thirty of the pages. I went back through, page by page, and read some of what I'd underlined and noted.

<u>None but those who have experienced them can</u>

conceive of the enticements of science. This struck me as very interesting, having just spent all day reading about Newton, Hooke and Boyle.

I shunned my fellow creatures as if I were guilty of a crime.

I can relate, Dr Frankenstein.

Two years after making the monster, Frankenstein discovers it has killed his brother. This is when the doctor starts to really go nuts. In the margin I wrote: Had he never considered what the creature might do?

A darn good question, if I do say so myself.

Later, referring to Dr Frankenstein's character, I scribbled in the margin: It sounds as though he is convinced justice will prevail.

It's questionable whether or not Dr Frankenstein was right about that.

I wrote all over this book in hundreds of different places, like the story and the questions it raised in my mind were too big for the pages to hold. These are just a few of my scribbles in the margins: What did he tell them? He has set his course on doom and power. The dead and the innocent, these are his obsession now. Was he never afraid? I am constantly afraid. Pastoral. This is the devil, I'm sure of it. He would commit another to the same misery. He has killed accidentally. The monster is innocent, because he has no remorse. The apple and the angel. Abandoned. Alone. Immortal. What's that noise?

When I look at the margin notes, I can see why some people might wonder about me. Maybe my parents are worried I'll grow up to be a reclusive weirdo who can't be in a room full of people without having his nose in a book or a journal to write things down in. And the strangest thing? I have no memory of writing these things. Maybe I did it at night, asleep, instead of trashing the walls in my room.

It's 11:30 p.m. Time to go online.

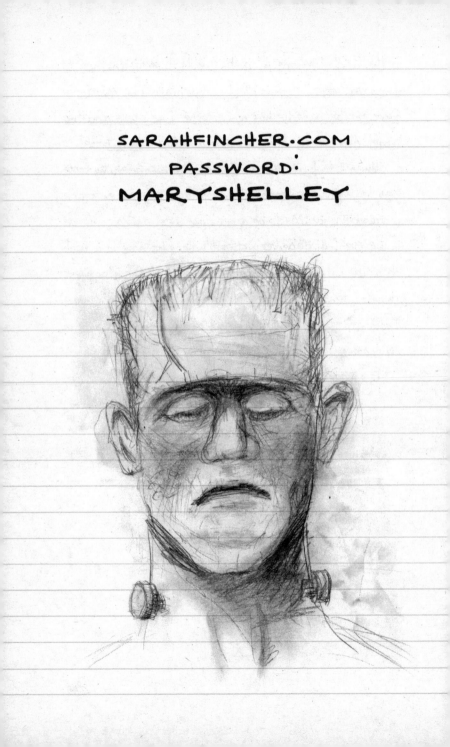

SARAHFINCHER.COM
PASSWORD:
MARYSHELLEY

Wednesday, September 22, 11:30 p.m.

Nothing. The screen is dead.

She's not there.

I wonder when my dad is going to sneak out and if my mom knows he's leaving.

He's going to leave soon.

He might already be gone.

Wednesday, September 22, 11:32 p.m.

Nothing's there.
This is starting to worry me.
Where is she?

Wednesday, September 22, 11:35 p.m.

Still no Sarah. Should I call someone? Maybe her camera's not working. I don't know what to do!

I'm checking my email.

Wednesday, September 22, 11:37 p.m.

She sent an email!

I don't trust maryshelley. Someone's been trying to hack into my site, in just the last few hours. Bonner? Your dad? My parents? Doesn't matter. Maryshelley is dead. I've beefed up security. Snoopers get shut out and hit with a nasty virus. Whoever it is won't be back. Lost a few minutes on this, so I won't be live until 11:40. Cutting it close!

Use theancientmariner

S.

I've got three minutes.

The Ancient Mariner. I was wondering when this was going to come up.

Sarah and I took the same English class together last year, and for some reason I obsessed over this poem. She hated it because it was so wordy and hard to understand.

But I loved it.

I think because it was so sad and lonely.

It's about how bad choices led someone astray. How he can't find home.

It's the story of a wanderer who lost his way and never came back.

I hear my dad sneaking down the stairs.

It's a ten-minute walk to Longhorn's Grange.

Sarah had better hurry.

Thursday, September 23, 12:42 a.m.

That's it. I'm calling the police.

Thursday, September 23, 12:43 a.m.

I can't do it.

I don't know why I can't call the police.

I just can't.

Who else can I ask for help?

I couldn't trust my dad even if he was here. And my mom? Either she's in on all this or she's totally oblivious. I can't bring her in. She'd go ballistic two seconds after I mention Sarah's name.

Henry. Henry can help me. He'll understand.

I'm going downstairs.

Thursday, September 23, 1:12 a.m.

Thirty minutes ago I crept down the stairs and stood in front of Henry's door. I stood there with my hand ready to knock and then the strangest thing happened. I heard the knock, but I hadn't moved my hand. This, I felt for a moment, was the final sign that I'd gone over the edge. Scrawling on my walls, seeing ghosts, and now I'm hearing myself knock without actually knocking.

The tap-tap-tapping wasn't coming from the door in front of me. It was coming from the door behind me.

The screen door that leads outside.

Something about that tapping made me want to run back upstairs and lock myself in my room. I couldn't turn around. Cold sweat started forming on my forehead. I could feel it, like blood about to drip from a dozen small cuts on top of my head.

It was either a big black crow tapping its beak on my front door, or it was Old Joe Bush. He'd finished off my best friend and now he was coming for me.

"Ryan. Is that you?"

I glanced around and saw a shadow in the doorway. Luckily, I knew the voice.

Sarah.

I have never travelled so quickly and quietly at the same time. Before I even knew I'd moved from Henry's door, I was outside on the porch, holding Sarah. She was shaking like she'd just fallen through ice into a frozen lake.

We whispered in the dark on the porch and I kept thinking my mom was going to walk up any second and catch us.

"I couldn't stand it in there any more with dead Dr Watts," she said. "Whatever was outside went left, away from the back door. So I went out into the night the same way I came in. I ran as fast as I could."

"My dad could be here any minute."

"I kept looking back, but there was nothing there. No ghost, just darkness."

Sarah was in shock. She wasn't herself. She was like a robot, repeating what she'd seen with this choppy voice full of air. She didn't understand we couldn't be there on the porch, holding each other.

"Sarah, my dad – or my mom, for that matter – we can't get caught."

"I'll make an anonymous phone call tomorrow from

the school about Dr Watts so someone finds his dead body."

"You're OK. That's the important thing. Can you make it home without me?"

I couldn't imagine getting caught. My parents had threatened over and over again to move away and leave Sarah behind if we didn't steer clear of each other. She had to go.

Sarah reached into the back pocket of her jeans.

"I think Dr Watts was planning to bring this with him to the Crossbones meeting. Hold on to it, will you? I think it's important."

I didn't want the envelope, but I had to get Sarah moving. My dad was going to appear out of the dark any second. I could feel him coming up Main Street. I just knew.

"Sarah, you have to go," I said, taking the envelope out of her hand and guiding her towards the porch steps. For some reason I felt like I was pushing her towards the edge of a cliff. I hadn't even noticed she had her camera with her. It was like an appendage, this metal whirring thing stuck to her hand. She carried it around so much I hardly paid any attention.

"I'll get my other camera from Longhorn's later, like around four, before it gets light outside."

I was concerned about her, after what she'd seen. "You should get some sleep," I told her. "You've been through a lot."

She looked back at me all glassy-eyed, and I thought she might tumble down the steps.

"Gladys, your dad and Daryl Bonner. Those three are all that's left. I wonder what they're going to say to each other?"

"You don't need to go back there tonight," I told her. "Promise me you'll get some sleep."

Sarah didn't answer me. She moved off and got swallowed by the darkness.

"Be quiet out there," I warned, maybe too late. "You might run into my dad."

Thursday, September 23, 1:31 a.m.

Timing is everything when you're deceiving your parents. If they show up at just the wrong moment, everything blows wide open. The close calls add up, until it feels like the end is inevitable. It feels like the truth is going to get out there eventually. The only question is when.

I made it upstairs with the envelope in my sweating hand without Henry opening his door. But when I turned to face my room at the top of the stairs, someone was standing in front of it.

It scared me so badly I nearly jumped down the stairwell and screamed for Henry to save me.

But then I realized it was my mom. Not necessarily a great situation, but better than having a killer standing in front of you.

"What's wrong with everyone in this house?" she said.

"I was just getting some water in the kitchen," I told her. (I hate lying all the time. It's getting way too easy to come up with what I need at a moment's notice. Lying on demand was never a skill I intended to cultivate. Honest.)

"Did you see your dad down there?" she asked.

And this is the timing part I'm talking about, because just then the sound of the screen door squeaking drifted up the stairs. My dad was home. And I could tell that Mom hadn't known he'd gone out.

She was his problem now, not mine.

"Get back in bed," she said.

I think she figured he and Henry had sneaked out to have some last-minute fun or something. It didn't matter to me. All I knew was the focus was off of me, I was back in my room behind my closed door, and I was holding an envelope that was supposed to arrive at a secret Crossbones meeting but never did.

Thursday, September 23, 7:15 a.m.

I had a terrible dream last night. Dr Watts wasn't dead. He was only sleeping. Sarah turned around and Dr Watts sat up. He'd been using the blue rock as a pillow and he picked it up and held it over his head.

"You're not allowed in here."

Sarah turned at the sound of his voice and Dr Watts bashed my best friend in the head with the blue rock. The blue rock turned red and I woke up.

I couldn't go back to sleep for a while. There was no noise in the house. It was crazy quiet, which always makes me try really hard to hear the smallest sound. It's a bad habit, because I do hear things if I listen too carefully. I thought maybe I heard my dad's whisper, closer than it should've been from under my door. And I'm almost sure I heard the sound of a marker writing on a wall. Maybe I was half asleep — I don't know.

I'm just glad it's light outside.

There's no word from Sarah, and I'm guessing she took me up on my recommendation and left the camera at Longhorn's and got some nerve-calming sleep instead. I bet she went home and collapsed and forgot to set her alarm. She must be exhausted.

Still, it bugs me that I haven't heard from her. I saw the ghost of Joe Bush just like she did. It was out there, away from the dredge. It's been in my room while I've been sleeping.

Of course, she's the one who found a dead body. Not me.

What if Sarah never made it home last night?

What if she wandered down a dead-end street and came face-to-face with whatever it was we saw on her camera?

I shouldn't have let her go out into the dark alone.

A real friend would have walked her home.

She's fine.

She's probably on her way to school, mad at me for not opening this envelope.

I was too afraid to tear it open last night.

I think I'll wait until after breakfast.

Thursday, September 23, 10:00 a.m.

I need to get a few timing issues down straight before I open the envelope. Everything is starting to feel connected.

OK, here goes:

Last night was Wednesday until midnight and then it was Thursday. The Crossbones met last night right after midnight.

Henry is scheduled to leave in a few hours, also Thursday. Things are going to get awfully quiet around here after that. Good thing I'll be back in school on Monday.

Another story ran in the paper this morning about burning down the dredge. They've moved it up again. It's now scheduled for "demolition by flames" on Saturday afternoon — two days from now, leaving two nights to visit it. After that, no one is visiting the dredge ever again.

I guess my point is that everything is converging. The Crossbones meeting, Dr Watts's death, the burning down of the dredge, Henry going home, the house getting quiet, me going back to school. Where's Bonner in all of this? I'm so sure he's involved in some sort of shady business with this whole thing. In fact, I'd bet my life on it. I can't wait to see what he says at the Crossbones meeting.

Now, to the envelope.

Thursday, September 23, 10:24 a.m.

I'm going to just lay this out there as straight as I can, because I don't know what else to do with information this important. What was in that envelope feels like the kind of stuff that could get me killed. Part of me wishes I'd never opened it and that Sarah had never found it. The other part of me is feeling like we're incredibly close to piecing together the hidden past of the dredge and that this is the most interesting and exciting thing that's ever happened to me. I think it might be even more incredible than Sarah and I could have imagined.

There were three pieces of paper in the envelope.

Meeting Notes

- Boyle's Formula

- J.B.'s trials
  and amendments

- Purpose of the code

- Systematic method for
  reclaiming the assets

CONTROVERSIAL "LOST" PAPERS BY BOYLE PUBLISHED

LONDON — British scientist Robert Boyle (1627–1691), regarded in some circles as the father of the scientific investigative methods employed by virtually all contemporary researchers, has had some of his most esoteric work come under close scrutiny with the publication of heretofore unseen works.

Revealing that Boyle spent many years dabbling in alchemy, these documents, to be published later this month by <u>Scientific Quarterly</u>'s prestigious book division, primarily concern themselves with the scientist's pursuit of turning gold into other precious and non-precious metals, and vice versa.

Reaction from British historians has been consistently negative so far, calling on <u>SQ</u> to halt publication in order to "Protect The Good Name of Sir Boyle."

Boyle's alchemical formula for separating and liquefying gold, as tested and amended by Joseph Bush and Ernest Watts, M.D.

Make a paste of equal parts antimony and stibnite, being careful with your hands and lungs. Deliquesce it, distill the deliquescence, and keep the liquid in a nonporous container (mind the alkalinity!). It will not keep its potency beyond 30 minutes, so work quickly.

Place the rocks or minerals that appear to contain gold in this liquid, and cover with a tight seal. (Be careful not to breathe the fumes at this stage.) After 20 to 25 seconds, open the container. The rocks will appear unchanged, apart from a dusty white coating, much like the coagula of dead ammoniac salt.

Move the rocks to a container of distilled water (must be distilled properly!) and the water will turn dark grey almost immediately. Wait at least 50 seconds (but no more than 80) and pour through a fine-mesh screen.

True gold will remain in the screen, in granular form.

Now grind a small measure of auric seed (granules) to a fine powder, add a drop of the liquid saved from the deliquescence process, and pour the gold granulate on top. The gold will liquefy on contact in working temperatures between 4 and 36 degrees Celsius, and remain liquid for up to 17 minutes. It can be poured into a mould in sections, as it is prepared, until the mould is filled. Wait 30 minutes after the final pouring before removing the block of gold.

So basically, while Robert Boyle was trying to discover a way to change gold into something else, he actually discovered something entirely different. This is kind of common in science, I guess, searching for one answer and stumbling on to another. Boyle never did figure out how to turn copper into gold or gold into iron, but he did figure out two other very interesting things. The first was how to quickly and easily separate gold from anything else, so that gold particles embedded in rocks could be freed and purified. Second, he figured out how to chemically alter gold in order to liquefy it without the use of heat, so that particles of gold could be liquefied and gathered together into larger units without a change in temperature. All of this was done through chemical alchemy, and all of it remained secret, even after the publishing of the lost Boyle papers. It was Dr Watts and Joseph Bush who thought to expand on Boyle's ideas and actually put them to practical use. Dr Watts conducted the experiments, and Joseph Bush wrote the paper and put the theories to the test within the dredge itself.

Clearly, Joseph Bush was a lot smarter than anyone imagined.

The papers give no details of the actual use of these

theories and practices, so I'm left to wonder about a lot of things. Did the secret society find out about these processes? Did Joseph Bush use the processes only to have other members of Crossbones turn on him? Did the members of Crossbones steal some quantity of gold from the dredge? If so, where did they hide it? And why are so many members of the Crossbones dead? Are they killing each other off in search of what — or where — Joseph Bush hid? Or is someone outside of Crossbones killing off Crossbones members?

One thing stands above everything that fell out of this mysterious envelope — the ghost of Joe Bush. It wants revenge, and for some reason it's turned its gaze on me and Sarah.

Thursday, September 23, 12:13 p.m.

Henry's gone, which bums me out.

Things are already getting quieter around here.

He said he wished more than ever that he could stay.

"I'd like to see them finally put an end to that thing. It's going to be quite a bonfire out there in the woods. I hope you've got a good volunteer fire department in this town."

This made me think of Sarah, since her dad happens to be a volunteer firefighter. He'll be standing there watching when it goes up. Him and all his buddies.

I wonder if they'll let me and Sarah go, and if they do, will we be able to stand next to each other while the phantom of Joe Bush gets burned into oblivion?

I say this as if he's not already dead. I wish he were alive so I could ask him a few questions.

"Tell Sarah to record it for me, will ya?" Henry asked as he gave me a good-old-boy sideways hug. He didn't seem to remember I wasn't allowed to see her. I think he was just holding on, trying not to get upset at leaving. A second later he was gone, big old cowboy hat and all,

heading back to New York. We wouldn't see him again
until next year.

To make matters worse, I still haven't heard from
Sarah.

I'm worried something might have happened to her.

But her parents would have called here.

She's at school.

She'll contact me this afternoon, I'm sure of it.

Thursday, September 23, 4:13 p.m.

My dad took Henry to the airport and my mom is at work. This house is SO silent. I took the envelope to the blue rock and left it for Sarah so she could read it. On the way back I stopped at the café for pie and coffee and stared out at the library for an hour. Then I came home, watched game shows on TV, and fell asleep outside on the porch sofa.

It's almost 4:30. I should have heard from Sarah by now. What's her plan to get the tape? What's she doing? Does she realize we only have tonight and tomorrow night and that's it? After that the dredge is gone, and all the secrets with it.

I'm tempted to call her, but that would be really dangerous.

I'll watch the History Channel instead. That'll kill an hour.

Thursday, September 23, 8:13 p.m.

This is driving me crazy. Why won't she call or email or throw a rock at my window? Nothing. Just dead air (bad choice of words). My dad and mom aren't talking much. They're taking a deep breath with Henry gone, trying to get used to the silence. Me? I'm smothered in silence! I can't take any more being alone and quiet all the time.

Thank God I start school on Monday. After that I'll talk to Sarah all I want.

We'll come up with something so my parents don't find out.

Thursday, September 23, 10:13 p.m.

Daryl Bonner just stopped by. That park ranger's got a lot of nerve. It's ten o'clock at night! Who stops by at ten for a chat on the porch?

I crept down the stairs so I could listen, because it occurred to me that maybe he had Sarah locked up or had heard something about her. Park rangers can't lock kids up, right? That's totally against the law.

Anyway, he didn't lock her up. But he was looking for her. I couldn't hear much, but I heard enough.

"With the burn day coming up, I'm nervous she's going to try to get back in there. Why? I have no idea. Just keep an especially close eye on Ryan, will you? I'm not saying he's going anywhere, but she might try to contact him if she's got some sort of plan that includes the dredge. I sure wouldn't put it past her."

"I'll keep an eye on my boy," Dad said. "You don't need to worry about that."

I felt like a prisoner under house arrest.

What gave him the right?

But I could see why my parents were so nervous. To hear it from Daryl Bonner, Sarah was completely out of

control and might drag me down with her. She was the
friend no parents wanted their child to have.

If only they knew I am just as involved as Sarah is.
She is out in the open, where everyone could see. But I'm
lying and sneaking around every bit as much as she is.

Friday, September 24, after midnight

She's out there tonight, doing something. I know it. She's in Longhorn's or Dr Watts's house or the dredge.

She just doesn't trust me any more. Why is she holding out on me? Why not at least check in and say hello? I can't understand what's got into her.

I've never felt this alone.

Friday, September 24, 6:15 a.m.

Hallelujah — she sent me a video!

SARAHFINCHER.COM
PASSWORD:
GEORGELUTZ

Friday, September 24, 8:15 a.m.

Now I know why she was so quiet — and it's not because she was mad at me or had stopped trusting me. We're the same as before.

And the tape?

We have all the pieces now.

And she's right — this is our last shot.

I need to know: What is my dad up to? What was Joe Bush up to?

I have all day to think about what a nightmare this is going to be. Even Sarah looks frightened, which frightens me even more. I try to lie to myself. I try to think that maybe last time in the dredge wasn't as bad as I think it was. And there is this part of me that's so curious. What's hidden down there?

It could be something really important.

Like the evidence of a murder.

Or a stash of gold.

Friday, September 24, 8:23 a.m.

Nine hundred bucks an ounce. If there's even one pound of gold hidden in a cave up on the mountain somewhere, it's worth fifteen thousand dollars.

I wish I could trust my dad and my mom. I wish our park ranger wasn't such a creep.

But most of all? I wish there wasn't a ghost waiting to kill me when I get to the dredge.

Friday, September 24, 11:23 a.m.

Taking a nap since I'll be up all night.

Friday, September 24, 3:15 p.m.

By the way, that georgelutz password was a real find. Sarah really knows how to freak me out. The Amityville house was messed up. I feel like I have a lot in common with George Lutz. I know exactly how he felt.

Friday, September 24, 4:43 p.m.

Daryl Bonner just knocked on the door. I tried to act like I wasn't home, but he yelled my name and it startled me. Nothing like dropping a can of Coke to alert others to your presence.

"Come on out," he said through the screen door. "I just want a word with you."

I swear this guy acts like he's a police officer, which is maybe why I'm so confused about how much authority he has. I feel like he could haul me off to jail and get away with it.

Anyway, the Coke was fizzing all over the kitchen floor, so I asked him to wait. When I got out to the porch, he was standing with his hands on his hips, staring down Main Street.

"Tomorrow, things are going to get a lot safer around here," he said. "But tonight's a different story."

"What do you mean?"

"I mean Sarah. She's just crazy enough to try and go out there again. Why are you two so interested in the dredge anyway?"

Why would he think I'd tell him?

"We're not," I said. "We're just bored."

"I don't believe you."

"I'm not sure what you want me to say."

"Just promise me you won't go out there tonight. Can you do that?"

I am so deep in trouble that one more broken promise won't hurt.

"I promise I won't go out there tonight," I said.

He didn't believe me.

"Trust me, Ryan. You don't want to be anywhere near there tonight. Just stay away."

I could already imagine him giving this same lecture to Sarah. She'd go along, just like I did, lying through her teeth. What gave him the right to tell us what to do anyway? He had a lot of nerve.

I began to think Sarah's idea of going at 3:00 a.m. made a lot of sense. That's so late it's almost the next day. It was our best chance to get in quietly, open the secret room, and enter the five-digit alchemy code into the cryptix.

Friday, September 24, 9:43 p.m.

Dad and mom are home. They're sitting on the porch downstairs. I sat with them for a while and we talked about a few things. My dad was surprisingly chatty.

I really wish I knew what he was up to.

I really wish I knew he wasn't a killer.

Apparently, Dr Watts's body was found – I don't know whether it was because of a call Sarah made or if some neighbour came across him. Whatever the case, it's big local news. (In Skeleton Creek, any death is big local news.) Dad doesn't look too upset – but at the same time, he doesn't look too guilty, either. And in the video from last night, he hardly looked like he'd just killed a man. So either he's innocent . . . or he's an amazing deceiver. I want to believe the first. But I'm fearing the second.

They were a little nicer about Sarah and school for a change, like they knew we couldn't dodge each other entirely. A glance or a hello would be impossible to avoid. Their message was clear: <u>Just keep it to a minimum and stay focused on your work. Don't get tripped up. Come home right after school.</u>

I asked Dad what time they were burning down the

dredge and he said early, about eight in the morning. That bothered me a little, because it meant a lot of people would be out there at the crack of dawn to get a good seat and see the flames. We'd have to get in and out of the dredge fast.

I turned in for the night and left them sitting together.

So quiet, those two. I guess a lot of years married can do that to people.

But they seem happy, generally speaking. My dad, especially.

Like the weight of the world has been lifted off his shoulders.

Friday, September 24, 11:13 p.m.

New email from Sarah.

Saturday, September 25, 1:30 a.m.

The password, in case someone comes into my room and
finds my journal tomorrow morning because I've turned up
missing, is <u>fatheraristeus</u>. Just go to <u>www.sarahfincher.com</u>
and put in those letters — fatheraristeus — you'll find us.
There's nothing left to say.
It's time for me to go.

SARAHFINCHER.COM
PASSWORD:
FATHERARISTEUS

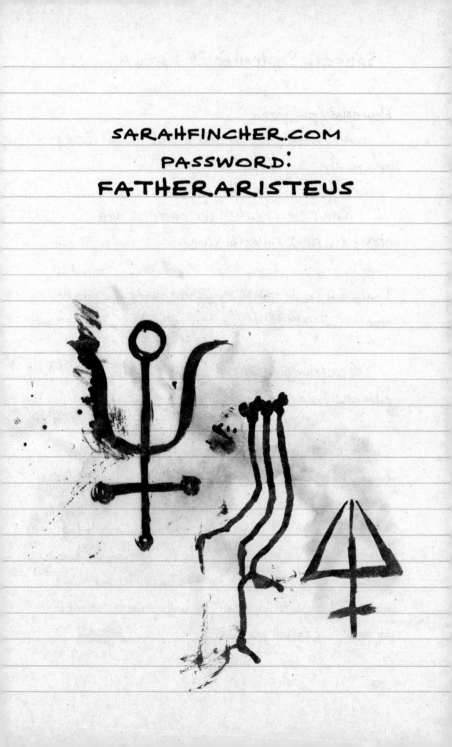

Saturday, September 25, 9:30 a.m.

It was Henry.

Bonner pulled off the mask and it was Henry underneath.

I didn't even realize the camera had stopped. I think I was in shock.

That's Sarah, writing in my journal. We're back home now.

Keep telling the story. Until I turn the camera on again.

The most interesting thing about the look on my dad's face when he realized his best friend was in the dredge at 3:30 a.m. was not his confusion. Sure, he was confused. Who wouldn't be? It was the recognition in his eyes that something was very wrong. It was the hint of an idea that Henry might have put me and Sarah at risk, might have even tried to harm us. The wheels were turning in his head, I can tell you that.

A son knows when his dad is on to something.

Bonner checked Henry's pulse. He was in bad shape, but he was conscious. His leg was shattered. I knew how Henry felt and how long it was going to take for him to recover. He was in for a long, painful ride.

When Henry glanced at the faces hovering over him in the dredge, he knew he was caught. Dad looked like he was going to kill him.

Henry lay there, broken leg and all, and started to deny, deny, deny. But my dad kept shaking his head slowly saying, "Just tell me the truth for once."

And that was it. Henry was ready for it to be over. He was finally ready for all the secrets to come out after twenty long years. Holding back that kind of tide must get very tiring.

Henry would say something, then my dad would fill in a blank, then me or Sarah, until all the parts were flying around the dredge, together in one place at last.

Henry was the only person besides Francis and The Apostle who ever saw Joe Bush move the lever and reveal the secret room. He discovered the secret room when the dredge was still tearing everything apart and forming Skeleton Creek. Henry had suspected the three men were stealing gold. Who wouldn't at least try? In fact, making sure gold wasn't being stolen was one of Henry's primary jobs on his frequent visits from New York. There was no way of knowing for sure how much gold should be coming out of the ground, which made it impossible to gauge with any kind of accuracy whether gold was missing. Henry had to sneak up on them, and that's exactly what he did.

In the middle of the night on a scorching-hot August 14 (even in pain, even so much later, he remembered the date), Henry got in the lake of water the dredge floated in, swam over amid the pounding noise, and boarded. Dripping wet from head to toe, he watched as Old Joe Bush moved a handle that didn't seem to have any purpose.

The thing that made me the most angry the whole time Henry was talking about this was that it seemed like he'd never, ever liked Skeleton Creek or anyone in it. From beginning to end, that had always been an act.

This, for me, was an unforgivable deception.

He only came back again and again for one reason.

You got it, Sarah. Gold.

It was only <u>ever</u> about getting his greedy hands on the gold.

But finding the secret room was only part of the puzzle. It would take a lot more than that to get what he wanted, because Old Joe Bush was a really smart guy who loved Skeleton Creek.

Henry didn't actually say this. We figured it out this morning. We haven't slept. And Ryan's dad finally started talking.

Yeah. Joe Bush created layers of secrecy within an organization he founded when the dredge showed up in town: the Crossbones. Its charter members were the three men who worked the night shift together on the dredge: Joe Bush, The Apostle and Francis Palmer. Only those three were aware of the location — or even the existence — of the secret room. The three were absolutely sworn to secrecy, and together they recruited Dr Watts, Gladys Morgan, and my dad, Paul McCray.

Dr Watts and Joe created the formulas for purifying and melting gold, but Dr Watts never knew anything about a secret room. He was content to do the chemistry with Joe and keep out of the dirty details of stealing gold. Joe gave the combination to the cryptix to my dad and Gladys but no one else. They had no idea a secret room had been created or even why. And everyone in the Crossbones was given one primary objective: to save the town from the evil of the dredge. In due time, when Joe was ready, all the members would know every secret. But he knew that would have to wait a long time, at least until the dredge was shut down for good.

There was one big problem. Old Joe Bush might have been smart as a whip, but he wasn't impervious to accidents. According to Henry (but then, how much can we really trust him?), Old Joe Bush really did die by accident. He really _was_ pulled into the gears by the cuff on his trousers. His leg was smashed and the gears spat him out into the water below, just like the legend said. And it happened the night after Henry discovered the secret room.

Only Joe knew every important detail: the existence of the secret room he'd made, where it was, the combination to unlock the cryptix, and the alchemy formula for processing gold the way he'd secretly done it.

Henry went straight to Francis Palmer when he could no longer turn to Joe for answers. He threatened Francis with losing his job. But Francis didn't know anything Henry didn't already know. He knew Joe spent hours and hours in the secret room. He knew where the secret room was. But that was it.

So Henry questioned Francis mercilessly and — as he told it — <u>accidentally</u> killed him. The same was true for The Apostle.

Henry said it something like this:

"They were all accidents! I never meant to hurt anyone. I scuffled with Francis up there and he fell. And that crazy Apostle, I dunked him in the river but I didn't drown him. He just slipped out of my hands and drifted downstream in the dark. It wasn't my fault he couldn't swim."

As far as Henry was concerned, very little was ever his fault.

After The Apostle died, the remaining members of the Crossbones fell quiet for years. Dr Watts, Gladys and my dad all went on with their daily lives. Between the three of them, they had no idea a secret room even existed. They only had a hunch there was some gold hidden somewhere and that someone had killed their friends in search of it. Best to leave well enough alone.

Year after year, Henry came back, searching for clues. He was sure there was a stash of gold hidden somewhere on the mountain, and he was convinced the cryptix contained a map that would tell him where to look. If only he could unlock it without blowing himself up.

On one of Henry's visits some kids were sneaking around the dredge and he chased them off. After that he needed a plan to keep snooping thrill-seekers away from the dredge. So he created the ghost of Joe Bush. Eleven months out of every year in New York gave him plenty of time to figure things out. Every year he added a few more subtle touches. Underground speakers, remote switches for sounds, iridescent masks and hoods, invisible trip wires that let him know when someone was heading down the trail towards the dredge. He even had his own secret shortcut through a seemingly impenetrable fortress of blackberry bushes.

Things were different with me and Sarah. Number one, we were persistent.

_I_ was persistent. What's this _we_ stuff?

Like I was saying, <u>we</u> were persistent. But there was one
thing that tipped Henry off that I didn't know about until
he mentioned it. Sarah had been going to the dredge and
filming it for weeks before that first video she showed
me. She'd already been inside, already scouted around for
hours. And here's one of the weirdest parts of the whole
story: Henry had surveillance cameras set up inside and
outside the dredge. Not only could he keep an eye on it
from a laptop he carried with him, he could also watch it
from New York. And watch it he did. Years of watching
the dredge turned Henry into quite the technician with
this sort of thing. If a person walked past certain places
in the woods on the way to the dredge, they unknowingly
set off alerts all the way out in New York. The best
I can understand it, there were wide pads buried a
foot underground and they were sensitive to pressure.
If someone walked on the trail, Henry knew they were
coming.

And so it was that by the time Henry arrived in
Skeleton Creek, he'd watched Sarah with her camera.
He'd seen her visiting the dredge not once but several

times, recording all kinds of things. It worried him enough to put his well-worn scare tactics into high gear when he showed up in Skeleton Creek.

Henry was also growing bolder because of all the talk about burning down the dredge.

He didn't know who else was in the Crossbones, but he was sure there were others. He'd seen little hints here and there from my dad. And there was that one night, when I fell asleep at my desk and woke up with words scribbled on my wall with a pen. I had that list — the list of everyone we'd discovered was in the Crossbones. It was that list that sent Henry to see Dr Watts when he said he was visiting a friend.

He had an excuse for that night, too.

"I didn't mean to kill Dr Watts. I forced my way in, that much is true. And I questioned him. I knew he had answers, but the old loon wouldn't tell me anything. I only swung one time, caught him right in the head. But he made me so mad, all clammed up like that. He was frail, more so than I realized. I'm sure he died of a heart attack, not that little bump on his head."

I guess you could say Henry's confession was tempered with quite a lot of excuses. At least he didn't do much complaining when it came to his own severe injuries.

"Did you write those words on my wall?" I asked him.

"What words? What are you talking about?" Dad asked. He was already mad, but the idea of Henry in my room, writing on my walls, brought his anger to another level.

Henry just looked down at his broken leg and wouldn't answer. He couldn't bring himself to look at my dad, and I never knew for sure if it had been Henry or not.

Finally, Henry just about passed out from the pain. Bonner called the hospital for an ambulance.

And I got the camera working again.

There was at least one more big surprise waiting for us on the dredge. But this part is better seen than said.

Wednesday, September 29, 4:30 p.m.

I'm back in my room alone. I began writing things down in here, so it seems like the most logical place to end up.

In some ways I'm more afraid than I was when this whole thing started. The danger had always felt as if it crept off the page of a scary story I'd made up in my head. Sure, it was spooky out on the dredge, but there was a feeling somewhere at the back of my mind that it was still a ghost <u>story</u>.

Things are different now.

Henry is out there somewhere. They searched the woods for days and found nothing. Chances are he planned for this and created a secret way to escape unnoticed. It would be just like him to think ahead. I wonder what his apartment is like in New York — full of cameras pointed at the dredge — watching them remove all the hidden treasures. I don't know and neither does Henry, because he's vanished into thin air. No one has been able to find him.

We've taken his gold and left him injured. He hates us. And the worst part, Henry thinks I'm the cause of all his problems.

From here on out the danger is real.

I'm going to change subjects because I'm hoping it will make me feel better.

Right after I pulled up that floorboard on the dredge and dumped the blocks of gold out, Daryl told us something we didn't know about his dad. Part of me feels like we should have figured it out on our own a long time ago, but we never suspected.

"You don't know who I am, do you?" he asked us.

It was Sarah who started chipping away at the options.

"You're not a part of the Crossbones. You didn't haunt this place. You've never been here before this summer. Who are you?"

"I've always suspected foul play," said Daryl. "<u>Always</u>. But I never imagined..."

"Who are you?" Sarah repeated.

"I was a foster kid in the city until I was twelve. That's when the Bonners adopted me. About a year after that I started going by my middle name — Daryl. I guess I was looking for a break with the past. A fresh start."

"What's your first name?" asked Sarah. She could

make a really good investigative reporter. Always first with the questions.

"Joseph," said Daryl. "I'm Old Joe Bush's son."

I remember feeling light-headed for some reason, like the ghost of Joe Bush had inhabited his son and we were about to be appropriately scared out of our wits. But the moment passed and I realized something as Daryl went on. The guy had lost his dad to the dredge. He'd obviously lost his mom young, too, and he'd been through the toughest kind of childhood. But curiosity had got the better of him. He'd been searching for answers just like we had, only the stakes were even higher.

"Now I know the truth," he said, looking at the opening to the secret room.

All this happened before we realized we'd basically forgotten all about the cryptix and the secrets we'd uncovered. After we figured out Joe had liquefied the gold and hidden it inside the planks of the dredge itself, Daryl piped back in.

"I should have guessed he would come up with something like this. My dad was about the handiest guy in town, everybody said that. That's why they chose him to run the dredge. He was gifted with motors and cranks and all kinds of machinery. But he was also a carpenter. A really good carpenter. He built the house we lived in. I remember him bringing these planks home, saying he was fixing them or replacing them. No one would have ever guessed differently. It was his job to repair things, and they were always just planks coming out of the dredge, so even if they checked, there was nothing to find. As far as anyone else was concerned, the dredge was slowly getting a new floor that always looked better and better. But when those boards went back, the centres were gone, ready to be filled with a block of pure gold. I guess my old man was pretty smart."

The diagram of the dredge we found in the secret room was very detailed. It showed every floorboard on both floors of the dredge. The ones Joe Bush had filled with gold were coloured in with a pencil. There weren't very many empty planks yet to be filled in. In other words, the dredge was a ship of gold. There were hundreds of hidden gold bars.

A year after New York Gold and Silver abandoned dredge #42 in Skeleton Creek, the town bought it for a dollar. There was some talk of turning it into a tourist attraction, but it never materialized. Who wants to walk way out into the woods and look at an old hunk of wood and metal? Nobody, that's who.

But it ended up being the best investment Skeleton Creek ever made.

I got an update from my dad when I came home today. So far they've pulled 1,400 pounds of gold out of the dredge. Every floorboard they pull up has another ten or twenty pounds of pure gold hidden down the middle. The price of gold is high these days, pushing a thousand dollars an ounce. My dad carries a calculator in his pocket, adding up the numbers over and over.

"At a thousand dollars an ounce we're at sixteen thousand per pound of gold," he told me earlier today. "Do you realize how much money what they've found is worth? Over twenty-two million bucks."

"It'll reach thirty million before they're done tearing it apart," I said. I'd studied the diagram carefully. There was a lot more to be found.

Thirty million dollars' worth of gold. Can you imagine? And it was always right there, sitting in the woods just waiting for someone to find it.

Even the dredge won't come out too badly in the end. There are already plans in the works to build a wood-plank trail from Main Street all the way out to the dredge with signs all along the way describing the amazing story Sarah and I uncovered, ghostly sounds and sites included. The fact that Henry has gone missing will only add to the urban legend and bring in even more tourists. Some people say they hope he never comes back and never gets found.

I am not one of those people.

There's talk of rebuilding the downtown and turning Skeleton Creek into a world-class fly-fishing and sightseeing destination, with the creek and the dredge as its centrepiece. Thirty million dollars ought to cover it.

My dad's planning to open a fly shop, since the town is "gifting" my parents and Sarah's parents five per cent of whatever comes out of the dredge.

Oh, and they're giving Sarah and me enough money to attend any college we want after graduation. We're currently on the hunt for a university known for excellence in both writing and filmmaking. I can only imagine what kind of trouble we'll get into when we show up on campus.

Everyone in Skeleton Creek seems to believe we can turn this place around. Still, for me, the town wasn't the most important thing the dredge gave me back.

What I got back, what really matters, is my best friend. They can have all the money as long as they let me and Sarah stay together, which it appears they are going to do. I suppose it would be hard to justify keeping us apart, seeing as how we saved Skeleton Creek and all.

I'm talking to my dad more these days, and he's talking, too. The fly shop will be good for us, a common interest we can share. Plus he'll be around a whole lot more, doing something he loves.

He doesn't talk about Henry. I can't imagine how it would feel for your best friend to betray you like that, to lie about so much for so long. It has softened my dad about me and Sarah, but he's going to have a hard time trusting like that again.

We've both learned a lot about the risks and rewards of friendship.

One of the nice things about being a writer is that writing is always there for me when I need it. During the past few weeks, through all the trauma and loneliness and fear, writing has been my replacement best friend. I've spent more time writing during the last twenty days than I did during the hundred days before that. Writing was a comfort. I feel I owe it something in return.

But the pendulum is swinging the other way now, and I suspect I'll be writing a lot less for a while. Sarah and I have some catching up to do. There's schoolwork. I'll be driving soon. I have a strong feeling Sarah will want to make a stab at locating Henry, and I can't let her do it alone.

But I know writing will be here when I need it, and this is a great comfort to me as I venture back out into the world full-time.

We're hosting a barbecue on the porch tonight, which means I have to wrap this up and go help my mom. Pretty soon Daryl Bonner and Gladys Morgan will be here along with a whole bunch of other town folks. Sarah will be here with her parents and her new camera. My dad will man the grill. Later on, when the bugs start hatching and the sun tips behind the mountains, I'll take Sarah to the creek so I can teach her how to cast a fly rod. Maybe we'll walk out to the dredge and take a look around, or up to Longhorn's Grange to retrieve her dad's ladder out of the tall weeds.

I can't help thinking about that blue rock we painted when we were kids and the simple question she asked me.

    <u>I want to paint the rock, don't you want to paint the rock?</u>

    Without Sarah, I'm no different than the legend of Old Joe Bush. I'm like a ghost, alone in my room, making up stories and keeping to myself. It's like Sarah has a hold of my hand, pulling me forward. She's looking back at me with the same question in her eyes over and over again.

    <u>I want to live, don't you want to live?</u>

    I do, Sarah.

    I do.

SKELETON CREEK

PRODUCTION TEAM:

Patrick Carman
Novel/Screenplay

Jeffrey Townsend
*Director/Editor/Visual &
Audio Effects*

Squire Broel
Producer/Art Director

Sarah Koenigsberg
*Production Manager/Director of
Photography*

Amy Vories
Lead Make-Up/Hair

Crystal Berry
Make-Up/Hair

Peter Means
Crew

Ben Boehm
Crew

Joshua Pease
Webmaster/Illustrator

Actors:
Amber Larsen
Tom Rowley
Jim Michaelson

Ghost Performers:
Jim Michaelson
Peter Means
Andrew Latta

Music/Soundtrack:
Portfolio Days

Publicity Video:
Peter Yenney

Craft Services:
Kept Man Productions

SPECIAL THANKS TO:

Rella Brown, Liaison for
Oregon Parks
and Recreation Department

The City of Waitsburg
Markeeta Little Wolf, Mayor

Cynthia Croot
Blake Nass
Brian Senter

Peter Rubie
Jeremy Gonzalez
David Levithan
Christopher Stengel
and everyone at Scholastic

GHOST IN THE MACHINE

PRODUCTION TEAM:

Patrick Carman
Novel/Screenplay

Jeffrey Townsend
Director/Editor/Visual & Audio Effects

Sarah Koenigsberg
Production Manager/Director of Photography

Squire Broel
Production Designer

Amy Vories
Make-Up/Hair/Effects Make-Up

Joseph Ivan Long
Stunt Coordinator

Dave Emigh
Special Props

Amber Larsen
Alternate Camera Operator

Peter Means
Crew

Nick Brandenburg
Crew

Katherine Bairstow
Crew

Joshua Pease
Webmaster / Illustrator

LOCATION ASSISTANCE:

Sumpter Valley Gold Dredge
Oregon Parks and Recreation Department
Miranda Miller, *Park Ranger*
Rella Brown, *Park Host*

Ashley and Brian Rudin

Walla Walla Elks Lodge - Russ Chandler

Sterling Savings Bank -
Connie R. Webb, *A.V.P.,
Branch Manager*

Waitsburg Four Mill - Mayor Markeeta
Little Wolf

Walla Walla Bible Center -
Pastor Dave Reed

26brix - George Davis

Merchants Ltd. - Bob Austin

CAST:

Sarah Fincher - Amber Larsen
Ryan McCray - Tom Rowley
Daryl Bonner - Jim Michelson
Paul McCray - Brian Senter
Gladys Morgan - Pat Yenney
Pastor - Ron Davids
The Apostle - Eric Rohde
Dr Watts - Mark Raddatz

GHOST PERFORMERS

Andrew Latta
Kevin Loomer
Joseph Ivan Long
Ben Boehm
Sarah Koenigsberg
Jeffrey Townsend

MUSIC / SOUNDTRACK

Portfolio Days

Ready for more brilliant Scholastic books?

It's the last dinosaur egg
on earth. How far would
you go to find it?

Roland Smith

JUNGLE
HUNTERS

You thought they were extinct.
You were wrong.

PART BOOK, PART
GRAPHIC NOVEL...

YOU CAN'T ESCAPE THE
TERRIFYING WORLD OF
MALICE.